Beautifully Awkward

Candied Crush #12

Charity Parkerson

I0550515

Copyright

The scanning, uploading, and distributing of this book via the internet or via any other means without the permission of the copyright owner is illegal and punishable by law. Criminal copyright infringement, including infringement without monetary gain, is investigated by the FBI and is punishable by up to 5 years in federal prison and a fine of $250,000. Please purchase only authorized electronic editions and do not participate in or encourage electronic piracy of copyrighted materials. Brief passages may be quoted for review purposes if credit is given to the copyright holder. Your support of the author's rights is appreciated. Any resemblances to person(s) living or dead, is completely coincidental. All items contained within this novel are products of the author's imagination.

—Warning: This book is intended for readers over the age of 18.

Introduction

Lance has spent his life hiding in the shadows.

Slade has spent his life in the spotlight. They're

equally lonely.

As a private detective, Lance depends on blending

in. Never in his life has he wanted to stand out until

he met Slade. Slade is a rock star and is wanted by

everyone. Lance is no exception. Unfortunately,

Slade is also the most clueless person on the planet.

Lance doesn't know how to get Slade's attention

when the guy seems totally oblivious to Lance's

desire. The entire situation feels hopeless.

Between touring, recording, interviews, and just

trying to live, Slade is tired. He hasn't had a

personal life in longer than he can recall. He's had

one-night stands and quick encounters in the

craziest of places, but there has been nothing real.

He enjoys spending time with Lance, but he doesn't think Lance really likes him like that. Slade is kind of nerdy and awkward when he's not on stage. Men don't go for him unless they're celebrity worshippers. He doesn't stand much of a chance with someone like Lance. So Slade does what he always does when he needs a little extra help. He turns to his identical twin.

Nothing good can come of Cade pretending to be Slade to gauge Lance's interest, especially since Lance is a detective. Maybe this crazy plan will blow up in everyone's faces. That's a risk Slade is willing to take for a shot at love.

Chapter One

For the most part, Slade could go almost anywhere he wanted in L.A. without getting overrun by fans. Occasionally, he had to sign autographs or stop for selfies. Mostly, he got left alone. That was usually because people didn't notice him off stage. He could stand on stage in front of forty thousand screaming fans and rock that shit. Off stage, Slade liked anime and comic book conventions. He played video games under the username Slade95, as he had done since he was sixteen. Not much had changed at twenty-six. He had amassed a fortune and gone multi-platinum so many times, he had lost count. Otherwise, he was just Slade O'Neil.

Despite being able to visit almost any establishment in L.A., it was still easier to stick to certain places frequented by famous patrons. As much as he didn't mind autographs and selfies, Slade always had his head in the clouds. Awkward moments happened more often than not when people caught him off guard. Since Slade stuck to places where he knew he would get left alone, he was more than a little surprised to spot Lance Hughes at a table by the window in his favorite lunch spot. Lance was a private detective and sexy as sin. Tall, dark-haired, and green-eyed, Lance might not stand out to most. To Slade, he was like a blinking neon sign on the darkest of streets because Slade knew him. He had met Lance at the gym. They had been in the same yoga class. Lance didn't strike Slade as the type to do yoga, but Slade imagined he looked the same. The difference was that Slade never looked the part of anything he did.

His outside didn't match his inside. Lance was hardened on the inside and it showed. He fascinated the fuck out of Slade. Slade was giddier than he wanted to admit over spotting Lance. He bypassed the hostess and headed for the man who had captured his attention after a single meeting.

"I don't remember L.A. being this small. Oh, shit. I'm sorry," Slade said, stopping and righting the chair he kicked over at the table next to Lance's. The woman waved off his apologies.

Lance looked away from the window at the ruckus and met Slade's stare. If he was happy to see Slade, Slade wouldn't know. Lance's expression stayed completely free of emotion. "Slade. Hey."

It didn't matter if Lance wasn't happy to see him. Slade was thrilled enough for the both of them. He liked Lance a lot. "Hi. Are you having lunch?"

Fuck. He was dumb. Of course Lance was having lunch. The guy had a plate of food in a fucking restaurant, for god's sake.

Lance didn't call him on his stupidity. "Yeah. Do you want to join me?"

"Sure." Slade grabbed a chair and knocked Lance's water over in his excitement. "Jesus. Sorry. I didn't get you, did I?" A nervous laugh followed Slade's question. It wasn't like he couldn't see Lance mopping the water from his lap.

"It's fine." Lance motioned for the server. "He needs to order," Lance said at the same time as Slade said, "He needs more napkins."

Slade realized what Lance said and smiled. He knew Lance wasn't blind to Slade being a tragedy, but he never called Slade on his complete idiocy. "I'll have the bacon cheeseburger with the sweet potato fries and a Coke."

Lance curled his nose at Slade's order before quickly returning to looking as if he had no thoughts to share.

Slade wasn't having it. "Which part of my order didn't you like? Are you vegan?"

A smile snapped to Lance's lips. "No. I don't like sweet potatoes."

"I don't either."

Lance blinked. "Okay."

"They're a good source of vitamins for replenishing energy, which I need. If you put enough salt on them, they're tolerable."

Lance scowled. "Doesn't that defeat the purpose of ordering a semi-healthy side dish?"

Slade shrugged. "I'm a complicated human."

A bright smile exploded across Lance's face.

"You are that. What have you been doing since I last saw you?"

Slade fought the urge to sigh like a besotted idiot at Lance's smile. "I've been in the recording studio, working on a new album. What about you?"

"Just working some cases. I've missed seeing you at yoga."

Damn. He was just so sexy. Slade imagined Lance was straight. He looked straight. Slade didn't know what to think or how to ask. He definitely didn't want to blurt out that he kind of liked Lance before his food arrived. That would make for an awkward meal if Lance didn't like Slade in that way. Slade wasn't sure Lance even liked him as a friend. He tried keeping the conversation light as first his drink arrived and then his food.

"What type of cases do you work anyhow? I

know you're a private detective, but do you work for insurance companies or whatever?"

Lance sipped his drink before answering. "No. I mostly work for an attorney. You know, cheating spouses and whatnot. I also do some freelance work for the government."

While Slade ate, he hung on every word. He liked listening to Lance talk. He had a soothing cadence to his voice—like listening to a love song. "Is this what you've always wanted to do?" Slade wanted to keep Lance talking so he could keep enjoying the man's voice.

With a shrug, Lance's expression turned bitter. "Not really. I used to work for the FBI, but I ended up with some debilitating PTSD. Now I work at my pace and take mental breaks on my schedule."

Slade wondered what Lance had seen in his

days with the FBI. Lance truly got hotter by the second, though. He had worked for the FBI, for fuck's sake, and freely admitted to mental health issues. Goddamn. He was a communicator. Slade felt like he had hit the jackpot, but he still didn't know if Lance swung his way.

"What do you do for fun or to unwind?"

Lance didn't answer right away. He looked almost uncomfortable, forcing Slade to goad him. "Come on. I won't tell."

"Honestly, considering who you are, I feel a bit ridiculous for admitting that I like to play guitar."

"Do you sing too?" Slade popped some fries into his mouth as he waited for Lance's answer.

"Just when I'm alone. Obviously, I don't have your talent."

Without thinking, Slade rolled his eyes. "You

don't have to have songs on the radio to like to jam. Do you game?"

"Like on computers or systems? Or do you mean like *Warhammer* and *DND*?"

The fact that Lance knew *Warhammer* existed made him one thousand percent hotter. "Any of the above."

The server appeared before Lance answered. "Are we doing one check or two?"

"One," Lance answered before Slade could.

As soon as the server walked away, Slade cleared up any misconceptions about that. "I'll pay for lunch."

Lance's mouth lifted in one corner. "I asked you to join me. I'm paying." His tone had changed, turning deep and fascinating to Slade.

Still, Slade couldn't let Lance pay. "Seriously,

I've got it."

Lance didn't argue with him. "I tried *DND* in high school, but I'm not creative enough to come up with campaigns. As to computer games, I have a few." The server passed their table. Lance stopped her and handed her a card. "Put our meal on this, please. Thank you." He went back to talking like he hadn't overruled Slade on the paying for lunch thing. "*Warhammer* costs a ton of money, if you want to stay current, and I don't have the time to put together all those tiny models and paint them. I just never got into that. Plus, you need friends with similar interests for all that."

"Do you not have friends?"

The server handed Lance his card and the receipt. He glanced at it and scribbled the tip and his signature before answering. "I have adult friends.

They have their own lives and no time to do things with me."

Slade understood. "I have time to spend with you."

Lance stared at Slade for a second before glancing out the window. His gaze slid back Slade's way, as if trying to decide something.

Slade didn't give him time to come up with an excuse to run away. "Would you like to come hang out at my house?" Even though Slade knew he sounded like a kid, he had to ask. He didn't want Lance to get away.

A smile touched Lance's lips. "Sure. I'm free for whatever."

It was hard, but Slade came to his feet at a tempered pace and didn't knock anything over in the process. "Good. You can follow me."

He almost fell after pushing in his chair. Lance caught him. Slade bit the inside of his cheek. Lance's body was hard beneath his shirt—like he worked out. Slade quickly straightened away and headed for the door. He really, really wanted Lance. Slade honestly didn't think it would happen. It especially wouldn't happen if Slade couldn't stop tripping over his own goddamn feet. Life was hard.

*

Lance was supposed to be working. Leaving the restaurant with Slade—hell, having lunch with Slade—had meant missing out on taking pictures of men leaving the business across the street. He would have to go back tomorrow. There was no way he would miss a day with Slade. While Lance knew Slade was famous, he didn't listen to Slade's style of rock. In fact, he had never heard of the guy before the day they met at yoga. Lance's interest had nothing to do with fame. Slade was fucking adorable. His stylish blond hair and beautiful blue eyes paired with a body made hard by constantly running from one end of the stage to the other while singing... delicious. Goddamn. Lance would call Slade sexy as fuck, but "adorable" fit better, because Slade was the hottest of messes. He was an awkward klutz. The first time they met, Slade had almost poked Lance's eye out. Lance had to wear a patch over his eye for three days after a single encounter. But his attention had been caught. Lance had downloaded Slade's music and found a new love. He hoped he did an okay job of hiding his interest as Slade led him through the back door of a fucking estate. Slade didn't have a house. He had a village. The place was massive.

"Here's the kitchen," Slade said after they passed through the mud room. "Let's grab some drinks."

He grabbed a six-pack of soda from the fridge and kept going. They passed through a living area that showed the pool through a long series of windows. Lance tried not to look at everything at once. Slade turned down a hallway and into a bedroom. It was as big as Lance's entire house. "This is my room." The bed was like two king-sized beds put together. It was insane. Slade led him through another door inside his bedroom. It was like a miniature movie theater, except it had been made for gaming. There were computers and systems all connected to huge screens. He owned things Lance had never seen before in his life.

Slade handed him a red camo controller. "I

have other colors, if you don't like that one."

He was sweet. "This is fine. Thanks."

Slade wasn't quick enough to hide his sweet smile and blush before turning away. It hit Lance. Slade probably didn't have any real friends. He likely had to question the reasons for the friendship of every new person he met. Lance didn't know how to prove he only wanted to be with Slade for Slade. He sat down in one of the plush leather theater seats and decided to try.

Slade sat next to him. Their knees touched. Neither of them moved away. They chatted about bullshit between talking shit to each other while playing a shooter game. Lance lost more often than he won. Mostly because he couldn't focus on anything past their knees touching.

"Are you dating anyone?"

The question caught Lance off guard, but he didn't hesitate. "No. Not for a long time. I was living with a guy for a while, but he couldn't handle my anxiety-ridden ass, so he started cheating with one of his co-workers. What about you?"

Slade didn't look his way. He kept playing like he didn't realize how important this conversation was to Lance. "Nope. I'm gone a lot and I don't meet anyone who wants me for me." He flashed Lance a bright smile. "I'm not anything like what people are expecting."

Lance wanted to touch him. It was damn near to being physically painful how badly Lance wanted to run his hand up Slade's spine and draw him closer. He hadn't been lying. It had been a long time since anyone touched him, or he had touched anyone else. He forced his hands to stay wrapped around the controller. "I'm sorry. Before I met you, I had never heard of you. What are fans expecting when they meet you?"

Slade shrugged. "I guess they expect me to be the rock star full time, but this is me." He flashed Lance a smile. "A klutzy, nerdy mess who likes to relax when I have the time."

The klutzy, nerdy mess was exactly who Lance wanted. "What are you doing tomorrow?"

Slade shrugged. "Probably nothing."

"You should have lunch with me again," Lance suggested, knowing full well he had shit to do. "I could bring something here and we could do this again tomorrow."

A sexy laugh burst from Slade. "Do you really think I'll let you get away with paying for lunch two days in a row? We'll go somewhere. My treat. Oh," he yelled, waving wildly and nearly taking out Lance's eye again. "Have you ever been to Boca on Emerald Lounge? You need reservations, but it's totally worth it."

"I haven't even heard of the place before."

At Lance's admission, Slade slapped Lance's knee and squeezed. "I'll get us reservations. You have to try it."

"Sounds great." Lance tried to sound nonchalant. Inside, he danced the jig. Slade didn't know it yet, but Lance was sliding his way into Slade's life. He planned to stick around. Slade was as good as his now. Lance was alpha as hell when he had his sights set on someone. Slade had his attention.

Chapter Two

Lance: *I had fun today. Do you want to play online with me?*

Slade: *Yes. I did too. Just give me a few minutes to get logged in.*

*

Slade: *So were you just letting me win today, or what? You kicked my ass.*

Lance: *Nope. I was distracted today.*

Slade: *Sorry about that. I know I talk a lot.*

Lance: *Snort.*

*

Slade hadn't slept at all. Not only had he stayed up most of the night playing games with Lance, he had also obsessed about Lance until the sun rose. While he knew now that Lance was gay, he still didn't think Lance liked him like that. He genuinely believed they were on their way to becoming friends. Slade didn't want to fuck that up by making an unwanted move. He wasn't very good at this. On the road, people approached him. They didn't care about anything other than who he was, so Slade never had to make a move. This was different.

To make matters worse, Lance was waiting in the foyer to go to lunch with Slade and Slade was in his bedroom freaking the fuck out. He needed advice or help. Slade didn't deal well with relationship stuff. He didn't have that slick edge his brother possessed. The moment that thought entered his mind, craziness took hold. Slade rushed from his room and up the back stairs. He wasn't even sure if Cade was home. Slade banged on Cade's bedroom door a little harder than necessary.

24

When Cade opened the door, he took one look at Slade and became the amazing four-minutes-older brother that he was.

"Whose ass do I need to kick?"

A chuckle that sounded uncomfortable even to him slipped out. "It's worse than that."

Cade's eyebrows snapped together. "Tell me."

Words fell from Slade in a deluge. "There's this guy downstairs and I like him a lot. I don't know if he likes me like that, though. We're friends and I don't want to fuck up making a new friend. But you know me, I can't tell if he likes me as a friend or if he's interested. I'm really a wreck over this."

"I see that."

At Cade's observation, Slade bit his lip and his shoulders fell. He didn't know how to handle reality. He was a performer and nothing else. Real life was hard.

"What do you need me to do?" The way Cade asked let Slade know he would reluctantly do whatever crazy thing Slade asked.

"We have reservations at Boca on Emerald. Would you go with him and report back?"

For a moment, Cade didn't respond. When he did, he sounded exactly like he couldn't believe this was happening. "I take it I won't be going as myself."

Slade bit his lip again and shook his head.

Cade's chin tilted upward. He stared at the ceiling, as if begging the gods to explain to him why he had been cursed with Slade as his brother.

"Please?"

At his begging, Cade blew out a sigh and Slade knew he had won. "Fine. One lunch, but that's it.

No matter what I learn today, that's all. One lunch."

With a nod, Slade drew a cross over his heart with his finger. "Cross my heart. One lunch. That's it."

Cade stormed away and got dressed. Slade chewed his bottom lip and prayed he wasn't making a mistake. It was just one lunch date. Cade would find out the truth and make Slade look a little less tragic. It would be okay. By the end of the day, he would know if Lance wanted him. That thought made all the risk worthwhile. He hoped. Jesus, he was fucked.

*

Slade hadn't been quite ready to go when Lance arrived for their lunch date. As he hung out in the front foyer, Lance wondered if Slade had forgotten someone was waiting for him. Slade hadn't been wearing a shirt when Lance arrived. Lance had thought that was all Slade needed to do was to grab a shirt. Fifteen minutes had passed, and Lance wondered if he should leave. The only reason he hadn't was that Slade hadn't been wearing that shirt when Lance arrived. Goddamn. The sexiness. Lance couldn't shake it. Slade had this flat stomach that begged for someone to bite it. He was gorgeous. Lance didn't know how he had caught Slade's attention, but he planned to hold on to it.

Finally, he heard footsteps behind him in the foyer.

"Are you ready to go?"

The hair stood on the back of Lance's neck as he turned. He had no clue who this guy was, but he wasn't Slade.

"Go where?" Lance asked, trying to wrap his

28

mind around the odd moment.

"Lunch, of course."

It hit Lance. Whoever this person was, he expected Lance to think he was Slade. "Okay." Even he heard the confusion in his voice.

The guy flashed him a flirtatious smile. "I made our reservation for noon. I'll drive, of course. That way, you can't get away."

There was obviously a reason for this ruse. Lance wouldn't spend his day guessing, though. He would not be leaving this house with this imposter. If Slade didn't want to spend the day with him, he shouldn't have asked Lance to lunch. Lance wondered exactly how far this guy was willing to take this game. Lance got a little more pissed off by the second. He couldn't believe Slade would ask him to lunch and then send him out with some type of body double. This was nuts. It was bullshit. Lance was the right asshole to pick.

"We'll head out in a minute." Lance crossed the room and closed the distance between them. He hauled the imposter into his arms and kissed his neck. The guy didn't even smell like Slade. Lance was enraged. If Slade wanted to make a fool of him, Lance would show him a fool. Two could play this game.

The guy tried stepping back out of Lance's hold, obviously not getting paid enough for this. "We should probably head out if we hope to make our reservation."

Lance tightened his grip. "We have a few minutes. There's no rush." He kissed the guy's neck again.

"Whoa. Okay. We should definitely go."

Dark clouds gathered in Lance's head. His temper roiled. The guy tried again to step out of Lance's hold. Lance pressed his lips to the guy's ear. "We're not going anywhere until you tell me who in the fuck you are."

Lance swore he felt the guy decide to double down. His hands went to Lance's waist. He stroked. "I don't know what you mean. If you'd rather stay in, I'm down with that. We could head upstairs to my bedroom instead."

A chuckle that sounded evil even to Lance's ears fell from his lips. "What would Slade have to say about that?"

"Are we role playing? I'm into that. Let's go upstairs."

Lance leaned away enough so he could grasp the guy's jaw. He eyed the man's features. They were damn near an exact replica of Slade's, but his eyes were a slightly different shade of blue. This one also had a bitter edge to him. Slade was softer. Playful. "Slade's bedroom is on the main floor. I know. I've been in it." He tightened his grip. "So, again, who the fuck are you?"

A wicked smile touched the guy's lips. He looked like a naughty version of Slade. That didn't appeal to Lance in the least. "I'm Slade's twin brother, Cade. Slade likes you, but for whatever dumbass reason, he doesn't think you like him as more than a friend. He asked me to go to lunch with you to gauge the situation."

A snort escaped Lance as he gave Cade his space. "Idiot."

Cade shook his head. "I can't believe you knew immediately I wasn't Slade. No one can tell us

32

apart. I can't go anywhere without getting accosted by people wanting Slade's autograph."

They were a mirror image of each other, but Lance knew Slade. He had spent too much time memorizing the guy's every feature since they'd met a month ago. Lance didn't see any reason to hide how he felt. "You swept me up and down with your gaze when you entered the room. Slade doesn't look at me. You have a harder edge to you than him. Plus, your eyes aren't exactly like his. You walk with a slight limp. He walks like he's late to lunch with the Queen."

Cade's eyebrows were raised, as if Lance had said a bit too much.

"I'm a detective," Lance explained. "I notice things."

A smirk touched Cade's lips. "Sure."

Lance didn't bother arguing. He got the feeling Cade's disbelief had nothing to do with Lance's job. Lance had shown his hand. He had admitted to how closely he inspected Slade's every mannerism. "Where is he?"

"His bedroom."

Lance dipped his chin. "It was nice meeting you. Go tell Slade you assessed the situation and decided I like him, but don't tell him you've been found out. I don't like games. We won't be playing this one again."

Cade shrugged. "That's fair, but I expect a to-go box from Boca now. I got dressed and everything for this bullshit."

"Deal." Lance could agree to his terms. He didn't intend to make Slade pay for this insanity for long, but he would pay. Despite being thrilled to learn Slade wanted him, Lance was angry as hell that Slade had tried tricking him. Lance hadn't lied. He fucking hated games. All day long, he dealt with liars and cheats. He needed Slade to be different. Lance was ready for a good man. He was ready to get real.

*

Slade made his way to the foyer with his heart in his throat. Lance liked him. Cade hadn't even made it out the door with Lance before picking up the vibe Slade couldn't read. Slade wanted to dance in place. He was giddy and nervous. Butterflies fluttered like crazy in his stomach. By the time he spotted Lance waiting, he had to force himself not to launch into Lance's arms like a crazy person. He wanted to be touched.

A line appeared between Lance's eyebrows as

he set eyes on Slade. "Did you change?"

Fuck. Slade hadn't thought about that. "Yeah. You know me. I'm a klutz. Had to change."

Lance shook his head. "All right. Are you ready to go now or is the offer still on the table to take you to bed?"

Slade's heart skipped a beat. Cade had tried taking him to bed. What the fuck? That certainly explained how Cade had gauged the situation so quickly. Slade didn't know how to feel. On one hand, Lance had obviously responded in a way that let Cade know Lance was into Slade. On the other, Cade had propositioned his man. He felt kind of sick.

Lance didn't wait for him to find a response. "Never mind. We have reservations. You said noon, right? That doesn't give you time to do everything on your list of promises. I mean, I'm not easy, but you named a few things I'm interested to see if you can deliver."

Slade floundered as Lance rushed him out the door. He was... confused and enraged. So, so furious. If Cade hadn't wanted to go to lunch, he should have said so instead of making promises Slade's awkward ass couldn't fulfil. Slade wasn't like his brother. He would never list the things he wanted to do to someone's body. Slade wasn't a prude. He had let men pull him into bathroom stalls and fucked in back alleys. Slade had done things. This felt different. Lance felt special.

As they reached Slade's Ferrari, Lance crowded him against the driver's side door. Slade lost a hint of anger as Lance's large body molded against Slade. His mouth touched the shell of

Slade's ear. "I promise we'll make our reservation but tell me again. Tell me exactly how you plan to make me scream."

"Um." Slade's hands automatically stroked Lance's waist.

"Come on, Slade. Don't turn shy now. You were more than ready a few minutes ago."

"I'm not shy," Slade argued. "I just..."

Lance didn't back away. "You're just what, sexy? Surely you remember what you said five minutes ago."

Slade floundered. "Well, you know. My head is always in the clouds. I say a lot of things. What did I say that you liked the most?"

Lance kissed the spot beneath Slade's ear. Slade's knees weakened. He really wanted Lance. Lance's lips moved to Slade's ear. "You said you were Slade's twin brother Cade, and that Slade likes me, but he doesn't know if I like him. Spoiler alert. I like you."

Slade's heart dropped. Words failed him.

Thankfully, Lance didn't seem to want words. "I don't play games, Slade. This is the only time I'll say that. If you want to be more than friends, good. That's what I want too. If you want to toy with me, find someone else. I'm a grown man. I want grown man shit—like an honest fucking relationship. If you don't want that, say so now. I'm not finding myself with Cade every time you want to test me. I'm not an idiot. I can tell you two apart."

Shit. "I'm sorry." Honestly, he felt like an ass. "I understand if you never want to see me again."

Lance leaned away and stared at Slade with those amazing green eyes he couldn't get out of his head. "Did you listen to me at all?"

"Yes."

"What did I say?"

Slade lost control of himself. He kissed Lance. Actually, he shot forward and damn near knocked their front teeth out before backing away every bit as quickly. Before he could apologize, Lance was on him. His mouth opened over Slade's. Slade found himself in paradise. People didn't understand. Slade was loved by millions, but by no one. Everyone knew his name without knowing him. Most of all, no one touched him. It fucked with his head the way Lance kissed him. He kissed like he cared.

The air stuttered from Slade's lungs. "You terrify me." The confession fell from Slade's lips in a moment of pure vulnerability.

Lance stroked Slade's bottom lip. His gaze never wavered from Slade's mouth. "Why?"

It was too late to turn back now. "Nobody wants me for me, but I think you do. You have no idea how easily that could break me."

Lance brushed his lips across Slade's. "I don't want to break you. I just don't want you to want anyone else ever again."

Goddamn. That was bold—like his dick was big bold. Slade wished he had the same courage in real life that he had on stage because, fuck. Lance's confidence was sexy as hell. He was in so much trouble. Slade swore he could feel Lance stroking his heart, attempting to steal it.

Lance kissed him again, stealing his thoughts before pulling away. "Will you go to lunch with me now? I'm starving."

Absolutely. Slade would feed Lance so well, he would never want anyone else. That was the only plan Slade had. He was the live-for-today type. That didn't mean he wasn't nervous about what they would do after lunch. Fuck. He was a mess.

*

To be honest, the scariest thing Lance had ever done in his life—and he did a lot of shady shit—was get in a very fast car with a very accident-prone Slade. It went fine. The more time he spent with Slade, the more he realized he could read the guy. Slade was into nerdy shit and he was clumsy, but the clumsy part came in bursts. Lance would see Slade's mind floating away—like creativity carried him into the clouds. In those moments, everything happening in reality became secondary. He lived inside whatever world he saw in his head. Those were the moments he became a danger to everyone and everything around him. But when Slade focused solely on Lance, Lance was the one who lost himself.

Lunch had flown by in the blink of an eye. Lance had found himself blowing off another day of work to lose himself in Slade's attention. Being with Slade was surreal. People openly took pictures of them. No one tried hiding it. People stopped Slade and fawned. Countless people took their shot with Lance standing right there—like he was invisible. Slade always gently but firmly turned everyone down. In a way, though, Lance got it. Slade was special. Meeting him was once in a lifetime for fans. Slade was nice and patient. Lance found himself becoming a little star struck too in the face of so many people fawning over Slade. It was impossible to ignore that he had kissed a really

43

famous guy. He did not understand what he was doing beyond pursuing someone he desired. While standing at the driver's side of his truck, Lance fought the urge to keep pushing reality away to stay with Slade. He needed to work.

"I hate that I have to work, but I can't avoid it any longer. I keep pushing back the job I'm on because I can't drag myself away from you."

"I'm not sorry."

A smile snapped to Lance's lips at Slade's response. "Me neither. When can I see you again?"

"Whenever you're ready. I'm always around."

Lance didn't want to sound too needy, but he already didn't want to leave. He couldn't wait too long to see Slade again. "This job should only take a few hours. Maybe I can stop back by later and we can play something again tonight."

All hints of shyness bled from Slade's features. "Maybe I can come to you and you could fuck me."

"Or we could do that," Lance agreed before Slade changed his mind. He had never felt this much hunger. "I'll let you know when I get home."

Slade nodded as he closed the distance between them. Lance didn't hesitate to open his arms for Slade. This time, when their lips met, promise flowed through their kiss. Lance's chest felt heavy. He felt like they were headed places. Lance couldn't wait to find out where. He hoped to some place permanent. Lance was getting too old to mess with guys who wanted him as a pit stop. Plus, he really liked Slade. He wanted more.

"I'll hurry," Lance promised between kisses.

Slade nodded as he pulled away. His cheeks were flushed, and his eyes looked unfocused. Lance fought the urge to take him right where they stood. Desire crippled him.

"Be careful working. I'll look for your text."

Lance shot forward and stole one more kiss before jumping behind the wheel of his truck. He had to get out of there before he tanked his entire life for a few more minutes with Slade. Lance had neglected his profession too long. He was too needy. Slade was too sexy. Damn. He couldn't wait until tonight. Lance was ready to start something new.

Chapter Three

Waiting for Lance to get home had Slade a mess.
Driving to his house felt almost surreal. Slade had
gone so long with nothing serious in his life. It
didn't feel possible now, but he honestly believed
he had met someone who wanted him for him. He
was fucking nervous—like about to go on stage
wrecked. When Lance's house came into view,
Slade barely noticed the white brick or well-
maintained yard. It looked like every other house on
the block. No doubt Lance purposely didn't stand
out. His job required someone who blended in with
the crowd. Slade no longer knew if Lance fit the
bill. While it was true Slade hadn't noticed Lance
until he had damn near poked the guy's eye out at
yoga, he saw him now. Lance was all he could see.

He needed to get to him.

Slade followed the driveway until he sat parked outside a detached garage beneath a security light. As he climbed from his car, a side door opened. Lance stood waiting. He looked sexy as fuck. In well-worn jeans slung low on his hips and a plain V-neck T-shirt, Lance looked lickable as hell. The light spilling out from inside the house looked like a halo, casting soft light on Lance's huge, hard body. Slade measured his breaths and pace.

Lance smiled. He looked genuinely happy to see Slade. His eyes lit from the inside—like he stared at someone he cared about. "Hey."

"Hey." Slade sounded every bit as happy to see Lance.

"Did you have any trouble finding the place?"

Slade shook his head as he headed for the door.

"Believe it or not, I grew up in a house about three streets over on Forrest Oaks."

Lance held the back door open for Slade as Slade closed the distance between them. "I imagine your parents have a much nicer home now."

"Not really," Slade said, trying to sound nonchalant. "They're dead."

Horror crossed Lance's features. "Fuck. I'm sorry."

Slade shrugged as he climbed the steps. "It was a long time ago. Car accident." he explained before Lance asked and the night turned depressing.

The moment Slade finally made it inside, Lance overcame him. He tugged Slade into his arms and covered Slade's mouth with his. Their tongues brushed. Hope kept crushing Slade's windpipe. He wanted this. Lance pulled away enough to whisk his

49

lips across Slade's one final time.

"Damn. I've been looking forward to that all day."

Slade's heart did a cartwheel in his chest. Lance always said exactly what Slade wanted to hear. Lance didn't give him time to respond in kind. He showed Slade where to leave his shoes before leading him into the kitchen. A candlelight dinner waited for them. The scent of delicious food filled the air.

"Wow. You've been hard at work."

Lance held a chair out for Slade. "Not really. I picked all this up on the way home. Cooking takes time and I wanted to see you as soon as I could."

Slade bit his bottom lip. He had been expecting to get carried straight to bed. This was nice. "Thank you. This looks great. Did you get what you were after at work today?"

The small square four-person table didn't allow for Lance to sit too far away, but Lance still chose a chair to Slade's left rather than sitting across from him. Slade loved that. Lance didn't answer Slade's question until after he sat and scooped some food onto Slade's plate. "Yes. Unfortunately, due to pending cases and whatnot, you'll probably get aggravated with me not telling you much about what I'm doing. Today is different, though, since it's likely already on the news." He gave Slade some baked chicken and mashed potatoes before working on his plate. "I've been watching that massage parlor across from where we had lunch yesterday, gathering photos of their clientele."

A laugh burst from Slade. "Is it a happy endings place?"

Something dark passed over Lance's features, and Slade's smile slipped away. "No. It's a cover for human trafficking."

"Oh." Slade had nothing. He had assumed Lance just caught cheating spouses and whatnot. He hadn't expected that answer. He had to say something. "Isn't that something for like the police or whatever?"

The haunted shadow tinting Lance's features lifted. "Yes, and no. There are several government departments involved with taking down traffickers, but they're still overwhelmed. It's not unusual for them to outsource some of the investigative process when they get tips. There are not enough people for all the tips they receive daily. So people like me do some poking around, freeing government agents to do their jobs more efficiently without wasting time on dead ends."

Slade ate as he listened. "How often does your part lead to finding actual trafficking?"

There was a hard edge to Lance, making Slade wonder how much bad he saw in the world. "Unfortunately, there are more hot leads than dead ends these days. The world is filled with the worst of people."

That was depressing.

Lance smiled. He visibly closed away the part of himself that dealt with the lowest of humanity. "I want to hear more about you. You have a twin. What's that like?"

If Lance needed happy talk, Slade would give it to him. "For me, amazing. I honestly have the best brother on the planet. He's my best friend. For him, it's probably not so great. Everyone always wants to know when he'll showcase his singing talent—like he's not special because he's not me. We've always stuck together, though. Every phase of my career, I've dragged him along with me. He believed in me when no one else did. I used to make him go on tour with me, but he doesn't like it, so I stopped." Despite his best efforts to stay upbeat, Slade's smile slipped away. "Honestly, that really sucks because it gets lonely as hell being on the road." He tried bringing back the smile. "But I understand. I'm busy and people were always mistaking him for me. Once they realized he wasn't me, they pushed him aside. He was always waiting on me to do whatever. It's not fair for him, so I won't ask him to go again."

Lance watched him a little too closely. He saw too much. Slade focused on eating. It was possible he shouldn't have said so much. "Does Cade know you're miserable?"

Slade picked at his food and avoided Lance's stare. "I'm living my dream."

"I know. That's not what I asked. I asked if Cade knows you're miserable."

A bitter smile tugged at Slade's lips. "Everything comes with a price, even living your dream. Maybe most especially living your dream. No one sees the long hours or the invisible chains sucking the creativity from my soul. No one understands the exhaustion or the passion driving me to an early grave because I can't stop. Still, I would die if this was gone tomorrow and I couldn't sing another note. Without music, I'm nothing."

Lance didn't look at him like he was crazy. In fact, his expression didn't give away any of his thoughts. "I've only heard a few of your songs and I didn't hear those until after we met. You're someone to me without the music, but I get what you're saying."

Slade wasn't as sure. Lance hadn't seen him lose himself to his passion yet. There was no Slade without music. Singing wasn't what he did. He was a singer. Those two things weren't the same. If no one ever listened to him again, Slade still wouldn't stop because he was filled with music. It wasn't his job. Music was his existence. His soul. Everything else was background noise. Nothing else was necessary. His gaze locked on Lance and didn't budge. Lance felt necessary, and that was odd. They hadn't known each other that long. That didn't seem to matter. Lance filled Slade with passion. He made Slade want to create even more music. He was magical.

*

Truly, Lance understood how Slade felt. His work wasn't artistic, but it was still a calling. He couldn't do anything else. Lance couldn't get up every morning and head out to something that didn't make the world different. People might not turn on the radio and know his name. But Lance knew the world was safer because of him, and he couldn't stop. His job came with a price, though. Lance didn't trust people. He had seen the worst of society and no longer believed there were very many good people left. Lance always waited for everyone's ugly side to show. He had seen too much, and that cost him dearly.

"Before this morning, no one had hugged me in ten months and one week." The way Slade looked at him kept Lance's confessions coming. "No one has held my hand in thirteen months and three weeks. I honestly can't recall the last time I took anyone to bed. My job is ugly, and it makes the world look cold. It's all cheating spouses and pedophiles. I don't look at people the same anymore. That doesn't mean I haven't been acutely aware of the loneliness. I like you a lot more than I've liked anyone in a long time."

"I like you too." Slade stood and held out his hand, as if he had waited all the time that he would wait to touch Lance. Lance pushed to his feet and linked his fingers through Slade's. Slade held Lance's stare with a confidence he rarely showed. "It's my job to hold your hand now." He gently tugged, urging Lance closer. Slade wrapped his arms around Lance's waist and squeezed. "I'll make sure you don't go without hugs." Lance's throat tightened as he held Slade against his chest. People really took for granted this part. Slade kissed his neck. "You'll definitely have to be the one who takes me to bed because I don't know where your bed is."

As much as Lance wanted to run for the bedroom, there was something else he wanted more. "In a minute." He tilted Slade's chin up and kissed him. It was soft and sweet. The way Slade's tongue stroked his screamed they had a future. For the first time in a long time, Lance felt hopeful. Then Slade's hand was inside Lance's pants and the mood shifted. His knees nearly buckled. He found himself rushing Slade down the hall and into his bedroom. Lance swapped between heated kisses and getting Slade out of his clothes. Lust tried crippling him when he caught sight of a few tattoos. Without his shirt and with his hair becoming a bigger mess by the second, Slade looked the part of a rock star. He belonged to Lance. Goddamn. It was humbling.

The moment they were nude, Lance urged Slade onto the bed before covering Slade's body with his. As their bare skin met, Lance hissed. He fully expected to fly apart at any second. The need to taste every inch of Slade overcame him. He kissed and bit his way down Slade's body until Slade's cock filled his mouth. The madness didn't ease. Slade gasped and moaned while pulling Lance's hair. Lance had never felt more powerful and wanted in his life. He licked and sucked, half out of his mind with desire. There were no thoughts left in Lance's head. Nothing mattered but the moment. He wasn't sure orgasm was even the goal. Lance gorged himself on human contact. He became a glutton, needing all the touches and tastes.

Lance moved away long enough to find his lube and the condoms he kept out of wishful thinking. Then he was back, sucking Slade's dick and toying with the man's asshole with lubed fingers. His heart required Slade's orgasm. He craved tasting Slade's cum. Slade writhed beneath him.

"Holy shit, Lance. Mhmmm. Goddamn." Slade openly fucked Lance's mouth and fingers. He was shameless as he visibly fought for release. Lance worked at getting suited up in between letting Slade fuck his throat and getting Slade ready for him. He became the multitasking master. Lance had no intention of losing his shot at being inside Slade. He wanted to taste Slade's cum, but his patience got thinner by the second.

"I need you inside me."

The words still rang in Lance's ears when Lance impaled Slade with his dick. Cries bounced from the walls as Slade's asshole tried sucking Lance's cock deeper. Slade scratched at Lance's skin as he came. Lance didn't slow. He pounded inside Slade, relishing every spasm. Lance immersed himself in the carnality of the moment. Everything disappeared as his muscles tensed. He held his breath while focused on the building pleasure. A cry tore from Lance's throat. He swore he died a little as cum poured from him into the condom. As he collapsed, Slade pulled Lance in for a kiss.

There was so much going on inside Lance's

chest. He had never felt closer to anyone than he did

Slade in that moment. It made no sense. Lance had

been in long, serious relationships before that

almost led to marriage. Slade shouldn't feel more

important than anyone ever had. He did. For

whatever reason, Slade felt like the one. How

utterly and completely terrifying.

Chapter Four

Waking up next to Lance fucked with Slade's head a little. He hadn't gone to bed and woken up with anyone in years. The way his chest and stomach felt couldn't be described. He wanted to keep Lance. For now, he knew Lance thought of them as a couple, but he hadn't suffered through dating Slade while Slade was on tour. Lance didn't realize yet how hard things would be. A small part of Slade didn't want to put Lance through that. But in the end, he recognized if he really wanted Lance, then he had to try. He had to give Lance the chance to decide for himself if life with Slade was something he could handle. Slade didn't want to get invested, in case Lance couldn't take it, but it was too late. He was attached.

His body stirred as flashes of their night together took control of his brain. He didn't know if Lance had been aware of how he looked at Slade while buried inside him. The possessiveness of Lance's expression stole Slade's breath all over again. For the first time in his life, Slade felt like someone saw him and wanted only him. He had to find a way to keep Lance.

Without thought, Slade dipped beneath the covers and slithered down the bed. He kissed Lance's stomach. Lance sucked in a sharp breath. Slade smiled at the sound. It felt evil. He kissed Lance's stomach again before moving lower. Lance's fingers dove into his hair. He held on as Slade shimmied lower. His tongue shot out, circling Lance's navel. Lance's erection grew. Slade urged Lance onto his back. When Slade had Lance where he wanted him, he settled between Lance's thighs and enjoyed himself. He played with Lance's balls and licked his shaft. Slade took his time savoring Lance's crown until he had Lance moving restlessly beneath him. Still, he didn't rush. Slade never got to indulge. If Lance wanted to be Slade's, he had to let Slade have some fun.

"Please."

At Lance's plea, something inside Slade broke. He sucked and bobbed, doing everything he could to make Lance blow. Slade rode the mattress and tugged at his cock, incapable of not touching himself in the face of Lance's open pleasure. Lance didn't hold back. He tugged Slade's hair, lifted his hips, and took what he wanted from Slade's mouth. Everything about Lance drove Slade wild. He couldn't stop trying to steal pieces of Lance by giving him more than he had ever had. Slade would spoil the fuck out of him. There was nothing he wouldn't do or give, as long as Lance kept showing him the attention and affection that had been missing from his life. As hot cum filled his mouth, Slade tugged faster, reaching for the same release. He cried out around Lance's dick as he ruined Lance's sheets.

As Lance dragged Slade up his body, Slade swiped his face across Lance's chest before Lance claimed his mouth. Their kiss was filled with so much affection and promise that Slade's eyes stung. He didn't understand where Lance had come from. In fact, Slade wasn't even sure if Lance would have caught his attention if Slade hadn't almost poked out Lance's eye at yoga. It was like Lance was proof of the divine. One small moment had changed the course of Slade's life. He didn't doubt for a second they had been meant to meet.

Slade's throat swelled. He would leave soon for four months to go back out on tour. That was a lot to ask from this brand-new relationship. He didn't know if they would make it. Slade had to try.

"Good morning."

Slade's heart squeezed at the sweet-sounding greeting. "Good morning."

Lance stole another kiss and smiled against Slade's lips. Something about that one small sensation had Slade all in. Whatever it took. They would make it. He was one hundred percent falling for this guy. There was no going back now.

*

There was no denying that getting woken by a blowjob was definitely the way he wanted to come awake every day. Lance kept telling himself not to get too attached. Slade would go back on tour soon and Lance would get left behind. When that day came, Lance would have to take it like a man. He had heard the love for music in Slade's voice last night. Lance would never try to steal that. So he would smile when Slade inevitably left him. He could settle for the now. Even a little time was better than nothing with Slade. Every day was a blessing. That was why he decided to ditch work again.

"What do you want to do today?"

With his legs tossed over Lance's lap and gaze locked on his phone, Slade shrugged. "If you're bored, I'm sure we can figure out something."

They had been snuggled on the couch for three hours. Lance felt obligated to point that out. "I'm not bored. We've been sitting here for a while. I don't want you to get bored."

Slade set his phone aside and focused on Lance. "It might sound crazy, but this is what I want to do. I don't get a lot of time to do nothing, and I get even less of this." He tucked in the blanket across them, snuggling closer. "People take quiet days for granted."

Lance agreed. He had spent many days running himself ragged just trying to avoid being alone in the quiet. Having someone to sit with peacefully was priceless.

"I'm happy if you are."

After flashing him a sweet smile, Slade went back to playing on his phone and Lance went back to staring at him.

Lance couldn't take the silence. "I know you mentioned at some point that you're going on tour again soon."

Slade nodded. "Just a short one in three weeks."

"What's considered short?"

The way Slade met his stare again left no doubt that Lance wouldn't like the answer. "Four months."

He tried to keep his feelings hidden. "I'm sure you're ready to get back out there."

Slade shifted positions and straddled Lance's hips. It was obvious he hadn't fooled Slade with his bland tone. "Don't worry. I can fly by sometimes to see you. Maybe, if you're interested, I can send you a ticket to meet me."

The pressure in Lance's chest eased a hair. "Sounds good to me. You don't have to send me a ticket, though. Just let me know when and where and I'm there."

"You'll get tired of being with me. Everyone does. I'm inconvenient." Slade looked so sad and sure as he said the words.

Lance couldn't let that go on. "Don't compare me to any weak-ass men you've dated in the past. Unless you give me a damned good reason, I don't plan on going anywhere."

A sweet smile touched Slade's lips. "Do you know what we need?" He clicked around on his phone. "Pictures." Slade touched his face to Lance's and started taking pics on his phone. He took several from different angles and various poses before pressing his lips to Lance's cheek and snapping a few more. Lance turned his head and captured Slade's lips. Things turned heated faster than expected. In no time at all, Lance had his hands on Slade's ass, squeezing and dragging him closer. Even though he understood they hadn't been dating long, and they were still in that can't get enough of each other stage, Lance didn't think he would ever get enough. He was enthralled. Whatever happened next and wherever this was headed, Lance was there for it. He liked Slade. Lance didn't feel that way about many people. He had seen too much of the bad side of the world. Lance no longer believed the good outweighed the bad. Slade was different. He was one of the good ones. Lance felt that in his bones. He couldn't wait to see where they went next. This was the life he wanted. Happiness filled him to overflowing. Things were finally looking up.

Chapter Five

Lance: *Good luck tonight. I miss you.*

Slade: *I miss you too. Just four more stops and I'm home. Is everything going okay there?*

Lance: *Everything is holding steady. I'm just ready to be with you again.*

Slade: *Same.*

*

Slade: *Cade tells me you stopped by tonight and checked to make sure he was doing okay alone. Thank you for that. I'm not sure anyone worries about him except me.*

Lance: *I care about you and you sounded worried about him when we talked last night. I wanted to put your mind at ease.*

Slade: *Thank you. He scared me when he didn't*

answer my texts.

Lance: *I can't have you worrying. I'm here for you.*

Slade: *I miss you.*

*

Lance: *Maybe if you get bored later, we can meet up online and play games.*

*

Slade: *Sorry. I passed out after the show.*

*

Slade: *Are you mad at me?*

*

Slade: *Have you seen Lance? He's not answering my texts.*

Cade: *The last I heard, he had to stake out some place. Maybe he's just working.*

Slade: *Maybe.*

Cade: *Do you want me to check on him?*

Slade: *No. If he's not answering my texts because he's done with not getting to see me, I don't want him to feel guilty. I get it.*

*

Lance: *Hey gorgeous. I tried to call, but you're not answering. I'm so sorry I missed your texts. I lost my goddamned phone and had to wait until the store opened to get another one. Cade came by and now I feel terrible. I would never ghost you.*

*

Slade: *Damn, I loved seeing your face last night. I wish I could come home for more than one night at a time. I swear it won't be like this forever.*

Lance: *Would you stop? I'm happy. We're fine. I'd rather be with you part time than anyone else in the world full time.*

Slade: *Damn. I love you.*

Slade: *I shouldn't have said that via text.*

Lance: *I love you too.*

*

Cade: *Do you want to get some lunch? I'm bored as hell.*

Lance: *Sure.*

*

Lance: *You have no idea how much I wish I could be at your side tonight. I absolutely know you'll win every award.*

Slade: *Not every award. There are some female categories too.*

Lance: *Nope. I'm convinced those are yours too.*

Slade: *LOL! It's not too late for me to fly you in to be my date.*

Lance: *I know, sexy, but I still have to work today. Just a few more days and it's all you and me for the foreseeable future. That's why I'm so adamant about getting my schedule squared away. When you get home, I'm not doing shit but keeping you in bed for days.*

Slade: *Damn. I can't wait. Not getting to see you is killing me.*

Lance: *Me too, baby.*

*

Cade: *Do you want to come over and watch Slade win all the awards?*

Lance: *I'm working right now. What time?*

Cade: *Nothing really starts until about nine.*

Lance: *I can do that. I'll grab us some beer.*

Cade*: Cool. I'll order us some food. We can FaceTime Slade together after he wins.*

Lance: *I'm in.*

*

While clutching three golden awards to his chest, Slade felt lonelier than he had in years. The last time he had gone on tour had been bad. This time was a million times worse. He hadn't expected to meet Lance, but Slade also didn't think that was the only reason he felt lower than he had years. Slade was tired. He felt like he existed somewhere between wanting to create all the music and wanting Lance to come home to him every night. Slade knew most musicians eventually got to a point where they still released new songs but didn't do full tours. While he hadn't thought he was quite there yet, Slade thought he might be close now that he had gone four months without setting eyes on Lance except for one-night flybys and video chats. Slade wanted a real life with Lance. He worried nonstop that Lance would get fed up and move on. That was why Slade was headed home two days early by private jet in the middle of the night. He couldn't stand another second without Lance.

After finally making it home at four a.m. and leaving the awards on the table in the foyer, Slade dropped his bag and followed the sound of the television. His footsteps slowed as he cleared the living room doorway. Cade slept sprawled across the couch, snoring. Beer bottles and pizza boxes littered the room. Slade bit his bottom lip as his gaze moved Lance's way. Lance was kicked back in the recliner with one arm slung across his eyes. The TV still played the same channel that aired the awards. Slade undressed from the waist up, took off his belt, and set one knee on the chair. Even though he was super careful, since he knew how big of a klutz he could be, Lance startled awake. Slade shushed him as he climbed on top and settled into Lance's arms. With his nose buried in the crook of Lance's neck, Slade breathed in Lance's scent and closed his eyes. Lance kissed his forehead. He felt Lance smile against his skin as Lance wrapped his arms around Slade. Exhaustion hit like a two-ton boulder in the warmth of Lance's embrace. Four months of nonstop working caught up with him in an instant. He swore darkness welcomed him home.

*

Lance had to pee. Half his body was painfully asleep and still Lance couldn't have been happier. Slade was home. Lance wanted to jump to his feet and cheer like a schoolgirl. He had never missed anyone so much in his life. Slade was worth it, though. If Lance died from a blood clot or burst bladder, it was worth the price. He couldn't get enough of holding Slade. There had been so many sleepless nights since Slade left to go on tour. More times than he could count, Lance questioned if they would work. Then, when he had been at his lowest after Slade had left his bed once more to go back on the road, and Slade had confessed to loving him, Lance had known then that he had to keep holding out hope for them. While four months wasn't a huge amount of time, Slade had other men throwing themselves at him. Lance couldn't compete. Yet he had somehow won Slade's heart. Lance would fight to keep him. His arms automatically tightened around Slade. He was beyond happy to have him home.

Cade sat up and glanced their way. His hair

stood in every direction. A huge smile stretched his lips as he spotted Slade in Lance's arms. He motioned toward them and silently mouthed, "Do you need help?"

Lance knew he needed to take advantage while Cade was offering. He nodded.

Cade stood and then used his foot to lower the footstool of the recliner while Lance worked at rearranging Slade's body. Slade's eyes opened for half a second as Lance stood while lifting Slade into his arms before he was out again.

"Thank you." Lance kept the words low as he passed Cade and headed down the hall. He didn't want to wake Slade, but he also didn't want to piss himself. After getting Slade settled in bed, Lance ran to the bathroom. He nearly sighed once his bladder was finally empty. After washing his hands and face, Lance made his way back to the bedroom. He spent some time watching Slade sleep. There were dark circles under his eyes, and it was obvious he had lost weight. Slade looked beyond exhausted. He needed every second of sleep Lance could give him. Lance stripped and climbed into bed beside him. Lance might not have much to offer Slade, but he could give him peace. The instant Lance settled in next to Slade, Slade rolled. He threw one leg over Lance and used Lance's chest as a pillow. With a smile in his heart and the entire world in his arms, Lance closed his eyes. They would rest together. Lance needed his strength.

*

The sound of the shower running dragged Slade from the sleep of the dead. He felt rough. Everything hurt. The inside of his mouth felt like he had been licking envelopes for twelve hours straight. His head ached. Stretching didn't seem to help. Instead, his leg cramped. After several long minutes of trying to massage away the pain, his mind cleared a bit. Memories trickled in. He had come home early to be with Lance but had immediately passed out from exhaustion. It was always like this after a tour. Months of little to no sleep caught up with him at once. He had no idea how long he had been out. His gaze moved to the clock. It was eight. He didn't know if that was at night or in the morning.

Slade stretched again. Sleep tried taking him away without his permission. He fought it. It occurred to him he had fallen asleep in Lance's arms in the recliner. Now he was in bed and the shower was going. Damn. He had slept through Lance carrying him to bed. It seemed Lance intended to leave soon. Slade tried harder to stay awake. With a force of will he hadn't known he possessed, Slade pushed himself up until he sat on the edge of the bed. His head spun. Damn. He really felt terrible.

Once everything stopped spinning, Slade pushed to his feet and headed for the bathroom. He could see Lance scrubbing his hair through the glass door of the wet room. Slade made a quick stop at the toilet before stripping. He bumped his hip on the door frame as he joined Lance. No doubt it would leave a nasty bruise. Lance glanced over his shoulder as Slade molded against his back.

"He lives."

Slade kissed Lance's shoulder before responding. "Barely."

Lance turned in Slade's hold and eyed him a

little too closely. "Don't take this the wrong way, but you don't look so great."

Awesome. His outside matched his inside. "It's always like this. I'll live."

Lance pressed his lips to Slade's forehead and lingered. "It's hard to tell in this hot shower, but actually, I think you might have a fever." He shifted Slade in his hold. "Come on, angel. Let me get you clean before I take you back to bed."

Slade couldn't stop himself from pouting. "I just got out of bed. I came home early because I missed you. This sucks."

Lance made a soothing sound. "It's okay, baby. I'm not going anywhere. We'll get clean and then I'll take you back to bed. I'll hold you and we'll spend time together there. You need rest."

Even though Slade stood still and let Lance

wash him like a helpless child, he didn't feel better. Most likely, his shit mood was due to being sick. He felt worse by the second. But Slade didn't want to be sick, because Lance deserved better. Yeah, it was dumb to be upset over something he couldn't control. Knowing it was dumb changed nothing. Sometimes, it felt like Lance was always giving way more than he got in this relationship.

"I'm sorry. You deserve a better boyfriend."

Lance snorted. "You're the one I want, so be quiet."

Slade felt worse mentally and physically by the second. They were clean and Slade wasn't even turned on despite Lance's obvious desire. Lance didn't acknowledge his lust. Instead, he kept taking care of Slade. He dried Slade's body and carried him back to bed. Slade felt terrible. Sometimes, it felt like he would never stop failing Lance.

"I'm going to run to the store. Do you need anything?"

Slade shook his head. He wished he had the foresight to stop by a store before coming home. He should have bought flowers and wine. Slade should be the one spoiling Lance.

Lance tucked him in tighter and kissed his forehead. "Then I'll be back in a few."

Slade nodded. Exhaustion weighed heavy on his chest. He closed his eyes for a second and Lance was gone. He glanced at the clock. It was ten. Fuck. Somehow, he had lost two hours. Slade found his phone and texted Cade.

Slade: *Lance went to the store. When he gets back, will you take him to do something? I'm not feeling great and he deserves better than being stuck here waiting for me to be awake for longer than ten minutes.*

Cade: *Sure thing.*

After reading Cade's text, Slade clutched the phone to his chest and closed his eyes. He focused on his breathing. As soon as he was up and moving, Slade would do something huge for Lance. He didn't know what yet. Slade wasn't sure what Lance would let him do for him, but he would go big. A light touch brushed his forehead. Slade smiled.

"Hey, gorgeous. How are you feeling?"

"Tired," Slade admitted as he opened his eyes.

Lance stared at a thermometer with his eyebrows drawn together. "A hundred and one. Take these pills and drink this ginger ale."

Slade forced himself to sit up. He winced as he swallowed the pills. "Is this what you got at the store?"

Lance nodded. He looked concerned. "I also picked you up some soup. Do you think you could eat?"

Slade shook his head. "I just want to sleep."

Lance's expression didn't clear. "Okay. I also grabbed you this." He reached between his feet and grabbed a stuffed animal. He passed it Slade's way.

The backs of Slade's eyes stung as he settled back down with the fuzzy brown bear clutched to his chest. "Thank you." Slade's voice broke. He truly was sick. His emotions were all over the place.

Lance stroked his hair. "Cade wants to grab some lunch, but I don't think I should leave you alone."

"Go. I'll just be sleeping anyhow. You shouldn't have to sit at my side."

"There's no 'have to' about it. I want to be here for you."

Slade really was in love with this guy. "You can cuddle with me when you get back. I want you to go."

Lance nodded. "If that's what you want." He kissed Slade's cheek. "My phone is on. If you need anything, let me know. Okay?"

Because he couldn't hold his eyes open any longer, Slade closed his eyes and nodded. "I love you."

He felt Lance's lips shape into a smile as he kissed Slade's cheek again. "I love you too, baby. I'll hurry."

Slade barely heard Lance's words. The world slipped away again.

*

"It gets better."

Lance dragged his gaze away from the menu he had been staring at for ten minutes at Cade's comment. "What?"

"Living with Slade's highs and lows," Cade explained. "It gets easier."

Lance let Cade's words sink in for a minute before responding. "I was just wondering if I should take him to the doctor."

Cade blinked. "Oh. There's a celebrity doctor who comes to the house. I can't remember his name. Slade probably just picked up something on the road while his immune system was at its lowest from exhaustion."

"I'm sure you're right." Lance went back to staring at the menu. He always ordered the same thing. Cade and he had visited this same cafe a dozen times while Slade had been on tour. Lance got the impression that Cade was lonely. That was a sentiment Lance understood. Slade was home now and still Lance felt like an asshole for how unimportant he felt. He had gone into this relationship with his eyes open. Lance had known Slade would be gone a lot. There was nothing fair about his hurt feelings. Slade hadn't done anything wrong. Now he was sick, and that wasn't his fault either.

"You're not a bad person for feeling neglected."

At Cade's quietly spoken claim, Lance winced. He wanted to deny it because he felt like the worst person on the planet. Slade hadn't done anything wrong, Lance reminded himself for the millionth time. "He'll be better soon."

Cade ignored his observation. "I promise you he's beating himself up more than you ever could, because he doesn't feel well enough to spend time with you."

Lance felt worse by the second. He loved Slade. The way he felt wasn't fair. "I know. It's fine."

Cade nodded. His gaze stayed locked on Lance, seeing too much. He opened his mouth, as if he planned to say something before snapping his lips closed, as if thinking better of it. Finally, he smiled. "What interesting thing are you working on now?"

Lance accepted the change in topic. He already felt bad enough today. "You know I work for a lawyer and can't tell you that." Lance paused for effect. Cade always had a mischievous glint in his eyes that made Lance tell him things he shouldn't.

He gave in. "But some woman wants me to get pictures of her husband cheating so she can break their prenup. You know that's about ninety percent of what I do here in L.A. when I'm not doing side work for the F.B—"

"He'll never choose you over music," Cade blurted, cutting Lance off mid spiel. He winced as if he hadn't meant to sound so harsh. "I mean, he loves you. Hell, he loves me, but he's living a dream that very few people ever achieve. That'll always be first."

It should have hurt, hearing the truth from someone who knew Slade better than Lance ever would. Lance was oddly fine. "I know. That's okay. I don't need to be first."

Cade looked relieved. "Okay. I just needed to hear that you're fine. I like you. You're the first person he's ever dated seriously. I don't want you to get hurt. I don't want to be forced to take sides. You're the only real friend I have."

Lance liked Cade too. That was important, since he hoped they would be related someday. "I'm not that easy to break."

A smile stretched Cade's lips. "Good. Tell me more gossip about work. Spill the tea."

As Lance fell into old stories that didn't fall under NDA any longer, he hoped he hadn't lied about not breaking. He couldn't lie to himself. These last four months had been hard. He hadn't expected to feel Slade missing from his life every second of the day. While Lance didn't know if watching Slade leave for tour would get easier, the fact remained that he loved Slade. He wasn't ready to admit defeat. The good far outweighed the bad.

Lance's skin already itched to be against Slade's again. Sick or not, Lance couldn't wait to hold him. He couldn't wait to be back in Slade's bed.

*

Even though Slade had been awake for over an hour and he had gotten up to brush his teeth, he was back in bed. His energy level was stuck at zero. He had thought several times about texting Lance and apologizing for the millionth time. In the end, Slade worried Lance might get sick of that too. He had never felt like a bigger failure.

The bedroom door opened, and Lance slipped inside. He had a bag in one hand and a Styrofoam cup in the other. A smile stretched his lips when he saw Slade was awake. "Hey, gorgeous. I brought you something to eat." He set the cup on the bedside table as Slade forced himself into a sitting position.

"You have matcha tea and," he passed Slade a bigger Styrofoam soup cup, "loaded baked potato soup."

He was kind of hungry. "Thank you." He popped the lid as Lance passed him a spoon.

"How are you feeling?"

Slade shrugged. "Meh. How was lunch with Cade?"

"That was yesterday, baby."

Slade's shoulders fell. He had lost an entire twenty-four hours. "I don't know why you stay." He shoved a spoonful of soup in his mouth to stop himself from whining.

Lance lightly rubbed his leg. "Because I love you."

"I don't deserve it."

Laughter etched Lance's feature. "You're a bit

of a baby when you're sick, you know."

A smile tugged at the corners of his mouth. He supposed he sounded somewhat petulant. "I love you too," Slade said in lieu of whining.

With a shake of his head, Lance took the lid off Slade's tea and then checked his temp again. Obviously not liking what he saw, he gave Slade a couple of more pills to take between bites. Slade made it through half the soup before his stomach protested. Lance set it aside for him.

"Can we cuddle?" Even Slade heard the pleading in his voice. He couldn't help it. Slade was beyond ready to get back to normal.

Lance stood and peeled off his shirt.

Slade's gaze locked on Lance's solid chest and didn't budge. "You might want to lose the pants too."

With a knowing smile, Lance stripped off his pants too before crawling into the bed and settling down next to Slade. He lifted his arm so Slade could use his chest as a pillow. "Come here, sexy. I've got you."

Slade gratefully snuggled into Lance's hold. He nearly sighed in relief once Lance's steady heartbeat thumped against his ear. Slade stroked Lance's stomach. Lance had a light smattering of dark hair on his torso. Slade savored the sensation of the soft hairs beneath his palm. He couldn't stop petting Lance. Even as his eyes fell closed, Slade found himself stroking Lance. His hand slipped lower until he brushed the waistband of Lance's underwear. Lance's breathing hitched. Without thought, Slade slipped beneath the band until he could pet the soft skin of Lance's cock. He whisked his fingertips up and down Lance's length as he hardened. The repetitive motion against the buttery soft surface was soothing. He didn't have a goal in mind. Slade didn't rush or try jacking Lance's dick. He simply petted him, comforting himself.

"You're killing me."

At Lance's claim, Slade tried to force himself to be still.

Lance chuckled. "I didn't say stop."

A sigh of relief rang through Slade's head as he went back to toying with Lance's erection. For several minutes, he trailed his fingertips up and down. His breathing deepened as Lance's turned ragged. The cock beneath his fingers jerked and twitched as cum jetted from it. Satisfaction carried Slade into his dreams. He loved that he could please Lance without trying. It was okay to sleep now.

Chapter Six

Tonight was a rarity. Since being back from tour, Slade hadn't gotten to spend anywhere near as much time with Lance as he wanted. It was like the world conspired against him and tested Lance's loyalty—like with Slade getting sick and now always working. He tried like hell to pack as many magical moments—like this one—as he possibly could into the days he spent with Lance. It just seemed like everything always went wrong.

No matter how hard Slade tried tonight, he couldn't stop kissing Lance. Steam filled the entire bathroom. He could barely see his hand in front of his face. Still, Slade's lips kept finding Lance's. The pleasure was too much. Love filled him to overflowing. Lance was so sexy and strong. He easily kept Slade pinned against the shower wall as he lifted and lowered Slade's weight over and over on his dick. They were one. Slade always felt like he was home when they made love. No one else made him feel like this. They were perfect together.

In the last three months since Slade came off tour, things hadn't been perfect. This part had, though. Whenever they touched, Slade knew he had to find a way to make this permanent. Lance treated him like a king, despite Slade's constant failures. Since Slade was always busy, Slade failed Lance a lot. In his defense, Slade worked toward a long-term goal that would make everything better. Right now, though, he knew loving him was hard. That didn't stop Lance. He kissed Slade and made love to him like there was no one else for him. It was humbling.

Slade threw his head back and sucked air as

Lance hit at the perfect angle. "Fuck." Slade dragged out the word. "You feel so good inside me." Even Slade heard the deep growl in his voice.

"Then come for me, sexy. Trust me, I could fuck you all night, but I want to watch you come unglued."

Slade closed his eyes and focused on the building tension. If Lance wanted to watch him come, he would. Slade gasped as Lance massaged that inner button with his cock. Everything narrowed to a pinpoint.

"Fuck. You're beautiful. I'm not going to last."

Ecstasy exploded through him as Lance's words caressed his ears, even though Slade didn't understand them. His entire being was focused on the pleasure rocking his soul. Only Lance's guttural cries vibrating from the shower walls gave him any clue that Lance had barely held out for him to finish. Slade loved that sound. It was better than all the music in the world. His heart melted as Lance's lips met his in the sweetest of kisses. He had never known what it was like to be in love before Lance. While Slade was certain he disappointed Lance at every turn, Slade wanted nothing more than he craved spending every second with Lance, even the ones when they slept.

"I love you," Slade gasped between kisses.

Lance's lips barely whisked Slade's. "I love you more."

Slade's heart dropped into his stomach. In a small way, he knew Lance was being sweet. The problem was, he had a feeling Lance really believed that. Every moment of every day, Slade felt like he sucked at being Lance's man. He more than felt it.

He knew it. Before Lance, Slade had never had to keep anyone else happy. He hadn't been expected to split his time. Slade knew he was losing Lance. Tension filled the air every second lately, bringing them closer to the end. That couldn't happen. Recently, Slade had made a huge decision. All he had to do was get his life aligned to his plan. Then Slade would ask Lance to marry him. Everything was so close. All Slade needed was a little more time. He tried packing every second he spent with Lance with love, hoping Lance wouldn't leave yet. Slade would make them right.

Lance dried Slade's body with a soft towel. Slade studied his features. He was rugged and fucking sexy. He left Slade awed.

"I love you," Slade said again, incapable of putting his emotions into words powerful enough to make Lance understand how he felt.

Lance paused and met Slade's gaze. "I love you too. Are you okay?"

Words crowded Slade's throat and stuck. He wanted to say he knew he wasn't good enough to keep Lance, but he still wanted Lance to stay. Instead, he took the chickenshit way out. The way he always did. "Yeah. I just don't think I tell you enough how much you mean to me." He prayed Lance would say he understood.

Instead, Lance touched his lips to Slade's. "We have the whole night. When we get back from dinner with Cade, I'm snuggling the hell out of you. I hope you're prepared."

A smile snapped to Slade's lips. It came from the heart. There had never been any chance he wouldn't fall in love with Lance. When they were together, Lance gave him everything he had to give. He was in this relationship three hundred percent. It was beautiful.

They reluctantly stepped from the shower and worked on getting dressed. Slade had made reservations at an exclusive restaurant where they would be left in peace to eat. Since Lance wasn't the only person Slade loved that he was failing, he had invited Cade. He hoped a nice family dinner would give them time to talk. Life had been pulling Slade in so many directions, he hadn't gotten to hear about his twin's life. Slade wanted to know what everyone had going on and he wanted to finally drop his plans on them. Honestly, he was a little nervous.

Slade styled his hair. His cellphone rang. Slade's gaze flew Lance's way. He saw Lance's shoulders fall, but Lance didn't look his way. Slade's gaze moved to the mirror they shared. Lance's eyes were closed, as if he barely held his shit together. Even as Slade answered the phone, his gaze stayed locked on Lance's reflection. Slade told himself he was wrong. He hadn't seen what he thought he saw. It looked a hell of a lot like the final straw snapping Lance's back after months of waiting for Slade to love him the way he deserved. Slade prayed that wasn't true.

*

After having Slade home for three months, Lance wished he could say that he got to see Slade all the time now. That wasn't the case in any way, shape, or form. While they slept in the same bed every night, Slade was always gone doing interviews, special performances, or working in the studio.

Lance was sickeningly in love with a dream. There were some tremendous highs where Slade would swoop in and give Lance amazing gifts before taking his breath away. Then the lowest of lows would hit when Slade ditched him for some last-minute thing... like now. He already knew he had lost to whoever was on the other end of Slade's call.

Lance watched the light play across Slade's perfect features as he spoke on the phone. His chest hurt. He had never seen a more beautiful man. Slade made Lance's knees weak with just one glance. He wanted to kiss Slade, but he couldn't. As always, Slade was busy doing something else. Fuck it. Lance closed the distance between them and pressed his lips to Slade's neck. Slade tried to hide the sharp breath that escaped him. He tilted his chin up to give Lance better access. Satisfaction roared through him. They had been getting ready to go to dinner with Cade and were still in the bathroom together when the phone rang. It was the perfect place for Slade to get clean again once Lance made him dirty.

"I have plans tonight, Felix."

"Damn right you do," Lance growled softly as he went to work on the button of the pants Slade had just put on.

Slade stepped out of Lance's hold. "We've talked about this. I'm not spending every second of my life in the studio anymore."

Defeat washed over Lance. Slade's mouth and angry tone said one thing, but Lance knew he was as good as on his way back to the studio. He didn't even bother following Slade into the bedroom to hear the rest of the conversation. Instead, he brushed his hair and avoided his gaze in the mirror. Lance knew how he looked—like a neglected child.

Once Lance had done all he could do to avoid heading into the bedroom, he took a deep breath and stepped from the bathroom. Slade was angrily changing clothes while Cade stared at the opposite wall as if they had fought while Lance had been avoiding reality, and now they refused to look at each other. Lance already knew what was happening. He didn't even ask why Slade changed or when Cade had shown. Lance simply headed for the closet where he kept a few of his things and found a t-shirt. There was no way he would stay in a dress shirt now that they weren't going to a nice restaurant.

"Why are you changing?" Slade visibly tried reeling back his curt tone. "There's no need for you to change, baby. Cade and you can still go to dinner."

Lance tried. He really did. Words just leapt from his lips without thought. "Am I dating Cade or you?"

Slade looked as if Lance had slapped him.

Cade slinked from the room.

Lance took a breath and tried calming his anger. "The only reason we planned to go to such an exclusive place was so you wouldn't get overrun with fans. If you're not going, Cade and I can find a different place."

Slade crowded Lance's space. "I swear it won't be like this forever. It's crazy like this when I'm cutting a new album. I'm under a time crunch, and when they find issues, I have to fix them."

Lance had so many words to say that he had

none. There was so much resentment building that it choked him. "I know. It's okay. Don't worry about me."

Slade buried his nose in the crook of Lance's neck. Lance's eyes fell closed as Slade's lips brushed his skin. "I'm sorry. Just let me get this done and I swear I will be so clingy and present that you'll wish I'd go back to work."

Despite his hurt, Lance wrapped his arms around Slade and held on. He supposed this was all anyone ever got of a dream. Wanting more was a ridiculous fantasy that was slowly killing him. Slade's lips touched the corner of Lance's mouth. Lance turned his head, capturing Slade's lips. Their kiss turned heated faster than jet fuel on a bonfire. They always came together like an inferno, as if they hadn't just made love in the shower. Lance was already about to come in his jeans when Slade's phone rang again. With a growl, Slade stepped back and answered.

"Goddamn it, Felix. I said I was on my way."

Lance didn't wait around to hear the rest or to say goodbye. The hurt roared to the surface and Lance's feet moved without thought. He headed out, finding Cade waiting in the hall.

Lance didn't even glance Cade's way. "Are you hungry or would you like to find something else to do?"

"Let's just find something else to do." Cade sounded every bit as defeated as Lance felt. Lance couldn't even imagine. He had only been doing this with Slade for eight months. Cade's whole life had been in the shadow of Slade's whims. Lance didn't understand why he stayed.

After climbing into Lance's truck, they rode in silence. Lance didn't ask Cade what he wanted to do. He was too pissed off to think straight. With no plan in mind, Lance stopped at the closest liquor store, bought two hundred dollars' worth of booze, and headed home. He didn't drink and drive. Cade and he needed a night they wouldn't remember.

They were almost to Lance's house before Cade finally spoke. "You're done, aren't you?"

Lance's throat burned. He wasn't ready to say the words. "Please just tell me something about your life. I can't talk about this."

For a moment, they sat in silence. When Cade finally spoke, Lance found his eyes falling closed in shared regret. "I'm in love with someone who doesn't belong to me and never will."

"I'm sorry." Lance didn't know why he

apologized. He simply felt like they were the same. He was pretty sure Slade didn't really love him, and Slade would never belong to Lance. Not really. Slade belonged to the world. To his fans. Lance was no one.

Cade spoke, pulling Lance from his depressing thoughts. "It's no one's fault but mine. I make bad decisions because I'm lonely. Then I end up wanting more than I should."

Yes. That was exactly how Lance felt. When he had met Slade, he had been so goddamned lonely. It had been years since he had told anyone he loved them, and he had been watching his friend Matthew fall in love. Everything had been perfectly aligned to take him down. Now he understood real loneliness. It was being with someone unavailable to love him back. Cade was right. Lance was done.

The saddest part was that Slade probably wouldn't even notice right away. Lance truly was a nobody. Slade would go to the studio and end up staying all night. Tomorrow, he would repeat the process. God only knew how many days would pass until it occurred to him he hadn't seen Lance in a while. How sickening it was to love someone one-sided.

"Well, I intend to get completely shit-faced and forget for a little while. Are you in?"

"Absolutely."

Despite everything, a chuckle escaped Lance at Cade's enthusiasm. At least they wouldn't be alone tonight. That was something. Tomorrow, he would face the loss.

*

With every ounce of his being, Slade tried to stay focused on the road. No matter how hard he tried, his mind kept drifting back to Cade's angry tone and Lance's hurt expression. It was hard to believe his body still hummed from Lance's lovemaking while his heart ached from Lance walking away. He wanted to go after Lance and explain. Slade couldn't dodge work, especially since he had been the one who set himself such a harsh deadline. Lance's birthday was right around the corner. Slade needed everything to be aligned before then.

He parked outside the nondescript brick building where the magic was made and headed inside. Felix met him outside the sound room. His hair stood in every direction in a stylish mess.

"This better be fucking unavoidable, Felix. I've pissed off my brother and hurt my man to be here."

Felix ran one tattooed hand through his hair. His hardened, light blue gaze looked unaffected by

Slade's claim. "I figured you'd want your baby to be perfect. *Awkward Love* has some weird clicking sound throughout and the tempo is off in some parts. Plus, two other songs have some issues."

Goddamn it. *Awkward Love* was the song Slade had written for Lance. He couldn't let that one go out being anything less than flawless. Not to mention, he was extremely anal when it came to his music. He didn't want anything less than fucking perfection in his name.

"All right. Let's get to work. I want this to be the absolute last night I break plans with Lance. Too much more of this bullshit and he'll end up in Cade's bed. I can't blame him if he's there right now."

Felix's eyebrows rose. Something dark crossed his features. "That's an odd thing to say."

121

Slade imagined it sounded that way. Unfortunately, it was also an accurate thing to say. He had never expected to be such a failure as a boyfriend, but here he was—the ultimate piece of shit.

"Nonetheless, it's true. So let's try to get this squared away."

Felix nodded. "Okay. Fair enough. Koda is on his way to do backup vocals. Get your ass in the booth. I have a quick call to make, but otherwise, we're good to go."

With a nod, Slade headed inside the sound booth. He put on his headphones, shutting out the world and preparing to disappear inside the music. Slade knew Lance didn't see it yet, but all of this was for a good reason. Soon enough, all the aggravation would be worth the payoff. All he needed was for Lance to give him a few more days.

Slade planned to change his life.

Chapter Seven

Just as Lance expected, he hadn't heard from Slade all night. When he had taken a very hungover Cade home, Slade's car was still missing. Lance couldn't deal right now. His mind was all over the place. He decided to work to save his sanity. There was a guy he had been trying to catch cheating for a while. Lance had slapped a GPS tracker on his Mercedes a week ago. So far, the guy's car had only been at work or home, until today. It had been parked at Boca on Emerald for half an hour—the same restaurant he had gone on his first real date with Slade. They had been there many times since, so Lance knew from experience the place had very few places patrons could sit out of view from hidden cameras. Yet there were several places in the parking lot to take pictures without being seen. Lance was ready to put this one to bed. Not to mention, he needed to get back on his game. He had been spending too much time dedicating his life to Slade and Slade's schedule. Lance had bills to pay.

Ten minutes after the GPS notification, Lance pulled into the parking lot next to the guy's car, facing the building. He dug out his camera and zoomed in, searching the faces for the guy he had only seen in pictures. Lance knew he had the sun on his side. It was out of his eyes while blinding the restaurant's patrons. That, combined with the dark tint on his windows, made it unlikely anyone would catch him. In less than a minute, he had the guy in his sights. He snapped a picture as the man beside him leaned close to his ear. Lance held his breath and waited, poised to catch an image of the guy's date. Lance's finger automatically snapped the pic even as his breath caught in his lungs. It was Slade. Lance stared at the screen of his camera as he zoomed closer to Slade's face. Even though he was inside and shades covered his eyes, it was definitely him. A thousand thoughts ran through Lance's mind. He wanted to hope he misconstrued the situation. Then the guy he had been there to catch leaned over and claimed Slade's lips. Lance automatically took another picture. His body kept doing its job while Lance's heart shriveled and died. He took pictures until his hands shook too hard to take any more.

Lance never suspected. Each time Slade had disappeared, Lance had completely believed every word Slade said about working. He snatched up the file from his passenger seat. Lance hadn't paid a bit of attention to who he followed. All the cheaters ran together in his mind sometimes. To him, they were all the same. He checked the information. *Felix Sommerland, record producer.* Lance swallowed the bile rising in his throat and checked the images he had captured for any hope he was wrong. As he flipped from clip to clip, Lance couldn't lie to himself. They were in love... as much as two unfaithful bastards could be. In the last ten years, he had shown countless pictures to spouses, ruining their lives. This time, the devastation was his, and it was real. Lance wasn't sure he would survive. The shattering in his chest felt a lot like it would kill him. He had seen enough. Lance pulled away. leaving Slade behind. He had never been more done with anyone in his life.

*

Slade didn't know how he managed to make it through the entire night and—finally—finish his album. Every second of the night, Cade's angry accusations filled his head. When he had broken their plans, Cade had called him selfish and a narcissist. He had point blank asked if Lance and he were people Slade loved, or were they toys he kept to play with only when he got bored. Slade had been so angry, he couldn't even recall his retort. Then Lance had stepped from the bathroom and the devastation had been written all over his face. Slade remembered very little outside of the ringing in his ears and Lance asking if he was really dating Cade. Until that moment, it hadn't occurred to Slade that maybe he was pushing Lance into Cade's arms. The worst part was, if it happened, Slade had no one to blame but himself.

Lance hadn't been waiting in his bed when Slade got home. Despite everything, exhaustion had won. By the time Slade realized he hadn't seen or heard from Lance in much longer than usual, he was in a full-blown panic. He tried calling and texting. His texts didn't show delivered and his calls went straight to voicemail. Lance didn't text him back or return his calls. Slade hadn't seen Cade to ask him about Lance, which had him worrying about two people. That concern grew into a full-blown meltdown when Cade also refused to answer his calls and texts.

With no other choice left to him, Slade headed for Lance's place. His truck was in the driveway, saving Slade from having his head explode. He practically ran to the door with zero fucks for his pride. The worst part was the fear Lance wouldn't answer. As he knocked, he wondered if Lance watched him through a window or the peephole with no intention of opening the door. He was almost surprised when the door swung open. His heart dropped when he saw Lance's face. There was no love or happiness. All the light that usually flickered to life in Lance's eyes every time he saw Slade was gone. Everything about him was hard—like Slade had finally managed to kill something beautiful.

"I'm sorry."

Lance took a step back, letting Slade inside. "For which part?"

Slade took Lance's willingness to talk as a good sign. He didn't miss his shot. "For canceling our date and pushing you on Cade. I'm sorry for every time that's happened."

Lance's eyebrows rose. "Is that it?"

Slade's mind raced. Was there more? Most likely, but nothing in particular sprang to mind. "Tell me all the ways I hurt you and I'll apologize for every single one."

Lance headed for the nearby table and picked up his camera. Slade watched as he turned it on and played with the buttons. Finally, he held it out to Slade. "How about if we start here?"

Slade grabbed the camera and checked the screen. His eyebrows rose. He flipped through each image, studying them. That was some tea for sure, but he had no idea why he should apologize. "I imagine Felix's wife will be really unhappy with this, but I don't understand why I'm apologizing to you for Cade kissing my record producer."

Lance snorted. "Are you really intending to

pretend to me you're not the person in these pictures?"

Slade was more than a little taken aback. He found an image that focused solely on Cade and held the camera out to Lance. "Cade has a tattoo behind his ear. I don't." He turned his head from side to side, showing no tattoo, while Cade clearly had a tattoo in the image.

Lance barely spared the picture a glance before setting the camera aside. He didn't look any less done with Slade. Aggravation boiled in Slade's chest. "I gave you proof that it wasn't me, and yet you're still looking at me like I could do such a thing."

"That's not how I'm looking at you," Lance said without missing a beat. "I'm absorbing the fact that I've spent so much more time with Cade than you—the man who is supposed to love me—that I easily mistook him for you. Maybe you didn't cheat on me and maybe I should be relieved, but I'm not, because you still cheated me. You stole eight months of my life, making me love someone who will never love me, and I'm pissed. There aren't enough I'm sorrys to give me back all the minutes I spent loving you while I only mattered if you had a minute to spare. I'm looking at you and I really want to take you to bed and let you hurt me some more, but I won't. I can't."

Slade wanted to scream and break things. He wanted to remind Lance that he had warned Lance that being with him would be this way. Unfortunately, Slade loved Lance. It didn't matter that Slade had told Lance from the beginning how things would be. Slade loved Lance enough that he wanted him to be happy, and Slade made him miserable. Slade could only give him his truth. "I was happy, and I was trying. You're breaking my heart right now, but I understand."

A bitter smile touched Lance's lips. "I'm glad to know walking away from me is that easy for you. That'll help me sleep tonight."

Slade snapped. "Are you fucking kidding me? None of this is easy for me. I've been fucking killing myself, working myself into the ground so I can finish my final album, fulfilling my contract. All so I could be free to be with you. So I could ask you to marry me and we could spend every second together. But no, I'm the selfish bastard who loved you enough to give up everything for you. Get fucked. I deserve better than this."

Slade didn't get a hint of satisfaction from

Lance's shock over Slade's meltdown or confessions. He was so goddamn tired. No one understood the absolute exhaustion. He didn't wait to hear Lance's thoughts. Slade was done with everything. He knocked a chair over as he left. Slade imagined there would be a huge bruise on his shin later, but now he felt nothing. Lance said his name, but Slade was beyond listening. He was fucking done. Slade had been giving everyone else everything his whole goddamn life. He was halfway home before it occurred to him that he was driving and should pay attention to the road. That was the final thought he had before the world exploded into pain and darkness.

*

There was a deep emptiness in the pit of Lance's stomach. It was so much worse than he could have imagined. He had never really thought about what it would be like to lose Slade. Not like this. Not so thoroughly and definitely not with it being his fault. Lance didn't know what to do now. His phone rang. Lance checked the face to see Cade's name. Lance ignored the call. There was nothing anyone could say to him that would make him feel even worse than he did now. He had lost everything. No doubt Cade had a lot to say. His phone alerted him to a voicemail. Lance swallowed past the lump in his throat. He didn't know if he should delete it or wait until he was a little more mentally stable to listen. Whatever Cade had to say, Lance deserved it. His phone chirped with a text. Lance couldn't stop himself from looking.

Cade: *911, bitch. Answer your phone.*

It started ringing again immediately. Lance

answered so fast, he almost dropped the device. "Hello?"

"Slade was in an accident."

Lance flew to his feet. He searched for his shoes before asking a single question. "What happened?"

"Apparently, he ran a red light and got hit several times. There's next to nothing left of his car." The way Cade's voice shook had Lance's fear through the roof.

"Is he okay? Where do I need to go?"

"I'm sitting in the ER waiting room right now. I don't know anything."

Lance crammed his feet into some shoes. He wasn't even sure they matched. "Which hospital? I'm on my way."

"Hold on. They just called my name. I'll call

you back in just a second." The call disconnected before Lance could beg for Cade to put him on speaker and let him hear the news.

Lance sat in the cab of his truck and stared at the face of his phone until he thought he might burst a blood vessel. He counted every second that passed. It felt like a million years crawled by. One minute turned into two. Two became five. Lance was so upset and enraged that he considered busting the window from his truck just to give himself relief. Cade hadn't even told him which hospital. He thought he would puke. Lance opened his browser and searched for any news online while he waited. An image of what was left of Slade's car popped up. Lance opened his truck door and threw up until he dry heaved. There was no way Slade had survived. There was nothing where the driver's seat should be. Tears streamed down Lance's cheeks unchecked. For the rest of his life, he would have to know the man he loved's last words to him were "get fucked." He would have to live with letting Slade walk away from him in anger. Lance would never get to apologize. He would never get to tell Slade how badly he wanted that marriage proposal. His heart was beyond shattered. It would never be repaired.

Lance's phone buzzed. He quickly unlocked it to find a text from Cade.

Cade: *Sorry. I'm not getting a signal inside the hospital any longer. They're letting me bring him home, but he can't be left alone. He's one huge bruise, has a concussion, and his nose is broken. I'm not joking when I say his entire body is messed up, but he's alive. Fuck. I feel sick. This is the same way our parents died. Meet me at the house. I'm sure you'd like to be the one who makes sure he doesn't stop breathing in the middle of the night.*

Lance: *I'm on my way.*

He had typed the words and hit send before he wondered if he should go. Lance was so fucking elated to learn Slade had somehow survived that horrific wreck that he had answered without thinking. It was more than possible that Slade didn't want him there. It was almost certain. The thing was, though, Lance loved Slade. Lance had been given another shot to make sure their last words weren't in anger, even if Slade still didn't want him anymore. Lance knew he would always need and love Slade. No matter what. He hopped from the truck and ran back inside to pack a bag. One bag turned into three as Lance found more and more things he would need for a long stay. He wasn't leaving until Slade was completely on the mend, even if Slade didn't want him anymore. If push came to shove, he would convince Cade to let him stay. There was no way he would walk away until his heart was satisfied.

He made it to Slade's house in record time. The gate was surrounded by reporters and gifts from fans. Lance had to fight his way through the security gate and then physically march two reporters off the property who slipped inside the gate behind his truck. Cade wasn't home yet with Slade. Lance used the time to take his stuff to Slade's bedroom and unpack. He planned to make it take as long as possible for him to gather his things and leave if Slade kicked him out. With that out of the way, he texted Cade to get an ETA so he could wait outside to stop more reporters from slipping in behind Cade's car. Every second that passed was torture. Logically, he knew Cade had already confirmed that Slade was alive. Lance's heart needed to set eyes on Slade. He needed to take care of him. Nothing mattered any longer. No fights. No hurt feelings. He loved Slade. At the end of the day, fuck everything else. Slade owned his heart.

Cade called as he approached the gate. Lance rushed outside to wait. He pulled security duty, muscling people back with smiles and a promise of an update later. Once he had the property secure, Lance rushed after Cade. He found him standing in the open passenger side doorway of his Porsche, chewing his bottom lip. At Lance's approach, he moved aside.

"Thank god. I don't know how to get him out

of the car. He can't move."

Lance looked inside the car. His heart stopped. He wouldn't have known it was Slade if he didn't already know. He wore hospital scrubs, making Lance wonder how destroyed his clothes had been. His face was completely unrecognizable between the swelling, bruises, and bandages. Every inch of bared skin was swollen and black.

With a breath for strength, Lance leaned inside the car and unsnapped Slade's seatbelt.

"Hey, baby," Slade said, sounding weak.

Tears filled Lance's eyes. He was barely holding his shit together. "Hey, gorgeous. I'm sorry. I don't know what else to do but to carry you inside."

Slade gave him a slight nod. "I have a lot of pain meds pumping through me."

Lance lifted him from the car.

Slade let out a scream that ripped Lance's heart to shreds. If he hurt this badly with medication, Lance couldn't fathom Slade without it. He moved as fast as he could through the house to Slade's bedroom. Cade rushed ahead of him. He pulled the blankets down so Lance could set him on the bed. Sweat coated Slade's skin.

Cade looked tired and scared. "I'll grab his stuff. He has a few prescriptions too. I'll get those and bring him something to drink and all that."

Lance reached out, stopping him. He gave Cade a quick hug. "Thank you. I'll keep him safe. You don't have to worry about losing him."

Cade gave him a sharp nod. Lance saw the tears in his eyes as he turned away. He understood. Things could have been so much worse. It was a miracle Slade was still alive. By the look of Slade, he likely wished he wasn't.

Lance immediately started fussing over him the second they were alone. "What do you need? Would you like me to cut these clothes off you so you can sleep nude? Do you need a sponge bath? Pajamas? Hard drugs?"

"These clothes are hurting me."

"On it." Lance didn't need to hear more. He found the scissors and sliced right through the material. He wouldn't torture Slade by making him move around to strip. Lance could barely breathe as he removed the strips from Slade. His entire body, every inch, was damaged in some way. "I can't believe the hospital sent you home."

"They wanted to keep me. I refused to stay."

It took every ounce of Lance's willpower not to

yell. Slade was so goddamn stubborn. "I guess it's a good thing you have me." He didn't give Slade time to argue with that statement. "What happened?"

Slade shrugged as Lance covered his nude body. "I don't remember. I don't even know why I was where I was when I got hit. The last thing I remember is being in the shower with you."

Fuck. Slade didn't remember their fight, or that they were over. Lance couldn't decide if that was a good thing. On one hand, that meant he didn't have to try to win Slade back. He could just pick up where they had their last good memory. On the other hand, if Slade ever regained his memories, Lance was fucked. He decided to skate the line.

"You had just left my house. I shouldn't have let you drive. You were tired, and we had a fight."

Slade stared at him through pain-filled eyes. "Why did we fight?"

Lance swallowed past a painful lump in his throat. "I accused you of cheating."

"Did you have a good reason to think I cheated?"

"Fuck if I know anymore." Lance's voice broke on the confession as the day caught up with him. He had almost lost Slade in every way.

Slade lightly stroked Lance's arm. "It doesn't matter. Will you snuggle with me? I'm having a hard time staying awake, but I need you."

Lance swiped away the tears leaking from his eyes and nodded. He gently crawled beneath the covers next to Slade. Lance tried to move slowly as he scooted as close as possible.

Slade cried out as he rolled to his side and into

Lance's arms. Lance's heart twisted in his chest at the way Slade gasped for air and his entire body shook from the effort of every movement.

"Let me know if I'm hurting you," Lance said as he held Slade.

Slade nodded against his chest. "I love you."

Lance didn't know if his heart would survive the day. "I love you too. I'm sorry we fought." Lance had to have his say now before Slade remembered anything. "I know you don't remember anything, but I'm sorry. You're the love of my life. Nothing means more to me than you. If I had lost you today, I would have gone with you. I'm not strong enough to live without you." Lance meant those words and not only in relation to Slade's near-death experience. He couldn't live with losing Slade. Lance had been angry. Slade had told him to

148

get fucked. But Lance hadn't believed for a second that they were really done. There was too much love between them for them to be finished. He had never thought they could end until Cade had nearly broken him with the news of Slade's accident. Lance had too much love left to give Slade to lose him. He would fix them.

"I'm not going anywhere," Slade said, sounding half asleep. "You're stuck with me."

Lance covered his eyes and fought a wave of tears. Too much had happened in one day, but he had been given a second chance. Lance wouldn't blow it. He couldn't. Slade was his entire world. Lance wouldn't forget again.

*

Everything hurt, including Slade's heart. Hurt was actually a vast understatement. Slade felt like he had been hit by a truck. Wait. He had been, and it was so much worse than that simple description. He would have had to have felt better to die. The pain was unimaginable, and that was while taking painkillers. Also, he remembered everything. Every tiny detail. Even while literally being crushed alive by his car, Slade had been set on repeat, seeing Lance's face as Slade had admitted to his exhaustion and broken them. In the moment the life had been leaving his body, Slade had realized that would be his final seconds with the man he loved more than life. Then he had somehow survived and Lance had shown up. Slade had seized his moment to cling to Lance. Now the pain kept him awake and overthinking. It was possible Lance was only there because Slade was hurt. Maybe once he got better, Lance would leave. He would recall all the times

Slade had chosen work. He had no way to know. Nonetheless, Slade could not tell Lance he remembered the way he had ended them. For now, Lance was here. Slade loved him too much to let go.

"You're not sleeping."

Slade didn't know how Lance would know with Slade's head on his chest. "I'm sorry."

Lance's hand lifted as if he moved to stroke Slade's face before thinking better of it. Slade fucking hated that because now he wondered if Lance didn't touch him because of the injuries or because Lance didn't think he had the right anymore.

"Why are you apologizing?"

There was too much to say. "Because I know I should be sleeping. God knows I'm so fucking tired that I want to cry, but everything hurts too bad. I'm a failure at even this." He hadn't meant to say that last part. His brain wasn't working properly.

He felt Lance holding his breath. "Why would you say that?"

Slade tried to use his faked amnesia to his advantage and say the things he should have before he pushed Lance too far. "I know I've been working too much. You deserve so much better from me than what you've been getting. I know all those things. I promise there's a reason for me pushing so hard. But maybe this wouldn't have happened if I hadn't been overdoing things. I know I'm a goddamned mess on the best of days. Why did I..." Slade started hyperventilating.

Lance slipped out from beneath him, making pains shoot through Slade. He bit his bottom lip so hard, he tasted blood. His vision blurred. Slade already couldn't breathe through his nose. Everything dimmed, going black. Slade wondered if he would die. It felt like the end.

Then Lance's lips touched his. "Breathe."

Slade sucked air.

Lance kissed his cheek. "That's it, angel. Please keep breathing. I love you. Don't do this to me. Stay with me."

Another inhalation filled his lungs. "I'm sorry."

Lance shushed him. "Stop, baby. Just breathe. I love that you're a mess on the best of days. You're beautiful in your awkwardness. I couldn't love you more. If anyone is to blame for you driving, it's me. I never should've let you leave. Please just stay and let me love you. I promise I'll take care of you."

Slade realized that not all the tears on his face were his. "I love you." The words forced their way from Slade's lips.

A stuttered breath left Lance, making Slade realize how hard Lance cried. That slayed Slade. Lance was strong and a guy's guy. Slade doubted Lance had ever cried in his life. Lance pushed from the bed and turned his back on Slade before Slade could see his face. "I love you. I'll fix you." Lance walked away on his promise.

Slade couldn't chase after him the way he wanted. The defeat had settled in hard by the time Lance returned. Slade hadn't looked at the clock, but he knew Lance had been gone at least ten minutes. Lance strolled through the room with something tossed over his shoulder. Slade couldn't move well enough to see what it was before Lance disappeared inside the bathroom. A few minutes later, Lance re-emerged and headed his way.

"Do you trust me?"

"Of course," Slade answered without thought.

Lance gave him a sharp nod. "Okay. I'm about to make you beyond miserable so I can make you better."

That didn't sound good, but Slade didn't have the breath to argue or respond as Lance lifted him from the bed. He carried Slade to the bathroom while inner screams tore through Slade's mind. Before Slade could grasp what was about to happen, Lance lowered him into the bathtub. It was filled with ice water. The shock stole his breath. His teeth immediately chattered. He felt like a million pins stabbed the surface of his skin at once. Slade wanted to scream, but his lungs refused to work. Then his body slowly went numb. He lost feeling in a painful sort of way. Oddly, it was a huge relief. Even an

155

uncomfortable numbing was a vast improvement over the way he felt before Lance had dumped him into the tub.

Lance eyed him while chewing his bottom lip. He looked like a scared parent. "Are you okay?"

Slade nodded.

Lance glanced at his watch. "Do you think you'll be okay if I leave you alone for a minute?"

Even as Slade nodded, he hoped Lance didn't plan to leave him alone as long as he had a minute ago. "I should be good."

Lance gave him a quick kiss. "Don't worry. I'll be back in half a minute."

"Okay." Even as he agreed, Lance lost even more feeling in his body. His teeth chattered harder. Still, he felt so much better.

Lance left him alone. He was gone longer than

half a minute, but not by much. When he returned, he had a thick, fluffy towel with him. "Okay. It's been ten minutes. Let's get you warm."

With Lance's help, Slade was able to stand. He was wobbly and couldn't feel his feet enough to walk, but his muscles didn't protest. For the first time since the wreck, Slade thought he might live. He wasn't screaming in pain. Everything was too numb to throb. The towel Lance used to dry him had obviously been warmed in the dryer. Slade's eyes fell closed in relief as Lance plucked him from the bathtub. As he carried Slade back to bed, Slade noticed Lance had turned back the covers and there were different blankets on the bed. He didn't recognize them.

Lance set him on the edge of the mattress and peeled away the towel. "We don't want this wet thing in the bed."

Slade's entire body shook from the cold. He didn't complain. Lance stripped, giving him something else to focus on other than the misery. Once Lance was nude, he lifted Slade back into his arms and climbed into bed. With Slade's help, he got Slade settled between his knees. Slade used Lance's hot chest as a recliner while Lance covered them both with the new blankets. They were soft and warm, making Slade realize they were heated.

"First ice, then heat," Lance whispered against his ear as he kissed it.

Slade closed his eyes. He took a breath. The shaking slowly subsided. The pins and needles stabbing his skin ebbed. He expected the pain to return, but it didn't. His body melded against Lance's as the absolute relief washed over him.

"There's still a thousand reporters at the gate. I had a hell of a time leaving to get the ice and blankets."

Fuck. Slade didn't want to think about that right now, but he recognized he had fans that worried. He would never completely belong to himself. It didn't matter how hurt he was. "Can you reach my phone?"

Lance slightly shifted before Slade's phone appeared in front of him. It had a huge crack in the screen.

An aggravated sigh escaped him. It was just one more thing in a long-ass day. Thankfully, the phone still worked. He had missed over a hundred calls and texts. Slade found a social media management app that he used to upload one status to all sites simultaneously. He made sure the camera was forward facing before he hit the red button to record a video.

"Hey guys." His voice sounded like shit. "I just wanted to let everyone know that I'm still alive. Obviously, I'm a lot worse for the wear and it'll be awhile before I'm running any marathons. But my man is here." He tilted the camera Lance's way until it focused on Lance behind him. "Say hi, Lance."

A sweet smile touched Lance's lips. He looked like someone had kicked his ass too, and Slade couldn't have loved him more. "Hi."

Slade brought the phone back to focusing on him. "Lance is taking good care of me. He'll have me back on my feet in no time. Until then, I probably won't be leaving my bed because—as you can see—I am pretty fucked up. Love you guys." Slade's voice broke a bit. He truly loved his fans and this life. His stupidity had almost cost him everything. "I might ask Lance to update all of you occasionally, but—for now—I need to rest. Thank you for everything." He blew the camera a kiss before shutting it off and hitting upload.

Lance took the phone from Slade and set it aside. His arms wrapped around Slade as his lips brushed the shell of Slade's ear. "Do you think you can sleep now?"

Slade nodded. His eyes were already falling closed. "Thank you."

He felt Lance's lips curve into a smile against his ear. "I love you, baby. There's nothing I wouldn't do for you."

There was nothing Slade wouldn't do for Lance either. That was why he had exposed Lance to the world as his man, and why, as long as they both lived, Slade would never admit he remembered breaking things off. As far as he was concerned, that never happened. He would do whatever it took to fix them, even if it meant he had to forget every word they had spoken in anger. As far as he was concerned, this morning had never happened.

Chapter Eight

Each day got a little easier in every way but one. While the swelling shrank and his bruises went from black to a nasty yellow, Lance still never touched Slade other than small kisses. They slept together every night. Lance never left his side or failed to tell Slade that he loved him. In fact, Slade enlisted Cade's help to secretly pay Lance's bills because he knew Lance's constant presence meant no money was coming in for him. Despite all Lance did, Slade still didn't feel very confident about their relationship. There was always a looming sense of dread. Slade didn't know how to fix them. He just wanted Lance to touch him with the same all-in passion as he had before. Now every touch was questioning, as if Slade didn't really belong to him.

Slade fucking hated it.

He decided to dip a toe back into real life and see what happened. "How do you feel about going out for lunch today?"

Lance glanced up from his phone. He eyed Slade, as if searching for something only he understood. "Are you sure you're up to that?"

Slade tried for a smile. He looked like hell, and he wasn't really ready for everyone to see him. That didn't matter. "I need to replace my phone, so I have to venture out anyhow. If I have to stare at this cracked screen much longer, I'll scream."

Lance pushed from the couch and shoved his phone in his back pocket. "I should definitely drive you then. You shouldn't be driving yet."

Side by side, they got ready to leave. Lance held his hand to keep him steady while Slade put his shoes on. It was nice. Slade didn't let him pull away as they headed for the garage.

"Do you have some place in mind for lunch?"

Slade shrugged. "You pick. There are a few good places near the wireless store."

Lance opened the passenger side door for Slade. Slade winced as he climbed into the truck. Lance watched him with an eagle's eye. "Are you sure you feel up to this? You could order a phone online and I could pick it up for you."

"You're not my assistant," Slade said, sounding angrier than he intended. Sometimes, the pain made him pissy. "I'm sorry."

If Lance was irritated in any way, his expression didn't show it. In fact, Slade couldn't read him at all. "Don't apologize. You're right. It'll probably do you some good to get out of the house."

Slade flashed Lance a grateful smile as he snapped his seatbelt in place. Lance closed the door. Still, his expression gave nothing away. Slade wanted things to go back to normal so fucking bad, he couldn't breathe half the time. Lance held his hand all the way to the store. That eased some of the pressure in Slade's chest. All the way through replacing his phone, taking pictures with employees, and signing autographs, Lance stuck to his side. They ended up going to the same restaurant they had eaten at the first time they had lunch together. Most people left them in peace. Only a few people approached them, and most only wanted to let Slade know they were glad he was okay. Lance stayed quiet through it all.

Halfway through their meal, the silence bested Slade. "We're never going back to normal, are we?"

Lance looked up from his food. "What do you mean?"

Slade shrugged. He felt uncomfortable now that he had said something. "You're unhappy with me. I suppose I should have let you go when you wanted to leave."

A deep line appeared between Lance's eyebrows. "What in the fuck are you talking about?"

With his heart in his throat, Slade held Lance's stare. "You tell me. You're the one who doesn't touch me unless I touch you first. You're the one who never looks at me anymore."

To Slade's surprise, Lance smiled. "Baby, I don't want to hurt you. You're still bruised from head to toe. I absolutely still want to touch you. You have no idea how much I want that. As to not looking at you, I didn't realize I wasn't, but it's likely because my heart breaks every time I see your bruises. I still feel like it's my fault."

"It's not."

They held each other's stare. Neither of them said a word until they broke simultaneously. "I need to tell you something," they said at the same time.

A chuckle escaped Slade. "You go first."

Lance looked uncomfortable as he set his fork aside. "I haven't been going to work. Mostly, it's because you need me, but also because I have to make a judgment call. You don't remember, but my last job was for a law firm client. I'm breaking my NDA, but that client is Felix's wife."

Slade fought to keep his expression blank. He knew where this was headed. "I'm not surprised. He's a shitty husband."

Lance nodded. "She wants to break her prenup because she believes him to be cheating. I have pictures of him with someone else. Now I have to decide if I want to get paid for that job or keep my loyalty to Cade."

Slade leaned back in his seat. He hadn't expected Lance to bring up those pictures again. Slade hadn't wanted to think about it. He could understand why this had been eating at Lance, though. It also explained so much about why he had been distant. "Run through both scenarios with me."

Lance looked relieved that Slade understood his predicament and took it seriously. "If I turn the photos in, she'll file for divorce and challenge their prenup. I would have to testify since I took the pictures. There would be no avoiding that. If I do nothing, I won't get paid and Felix gets away with fucking everyone over."

Felix had been Slade's record producer for years. He liked Felix, but they were still more of business associates than friends. While Slade had introduced Cade to Felix, he hadn't known they were seeing each other before Lance had shown him those pictures. Everyone knew Lance was dating Slade. If Lance testified, it would be a huge blow to Slade's career. The easy thing to do would be to do nothing. Slade hated a fucking cheater and Felix was stringing along Slade's twin while he had a fucking wife. It was complicated.

"What is your gut telling you?"

Lance's shoulders fell at the question. "I don't know. Cade had to know he's married, and you have to work with the guy. On the other hand, what a piece of shit."

"You didn't say anything about not getting paid."

Lance shrugged. "The money isn't as important as all the other factors."

"Maybe I could give you a third option."

A smile snapped to Lance's lips. "I'm definitely open to suggestions."

"Quit, marry me, and I'll anonymously send the pictures to Megan."

For a moment, Lance stared at him while looking blown away. "Are you serious?"

Slade nodded. "There's nothing I want more than to be married to you. I know life with me hasn't been easy, and I haven't given you any reason to want to be with me forever. That's what I want, though. If you need to think or whatever."

"Yes."

Confusion reigned. "Yes, what?"

"Yes, I'll marry you."

Shock had Slade slow on the uptake. "Really?"

Happiness nearly had Slade levitating in his seat.

"Yes."

Slade flew to his feet, knocking over their drinks and nearly pushing the woman behind him from her chair. He quickly apologized as he circled the table and tackled Lance. It hurt like hell on his sore torso. Every place the seatbelt nearly cut him in two screamed, but it was worth it. He also kicked over a chair and elbowed someone, but nothing could dampen his mood. Slade climbed into Lance's lap, pushing the table two feet in the process, making silverware rattle and their overturned glasses roll. He didn't care. Slade kissed Lance.

"I can't believe you said yes."

A sexy chuckle rumbled from Lance's chest. "Why are you so surprised?"

"Because you never touch me anymore," Slade said, admitting his fears. "I thought maybe you were done with me and you were just waiting for me to get better to leave."

"Oh, baby." Lance's fingertips found their way to bare skin at the edge of Slade's waistband. "Sleeping next to this sexy body every night and not being able to touch you has been torture. You're still in a lot of pain. I haven't wanted to make anything worse. That's it. That's the only reason. You're my everything, sweet baby. Of course I want to get married."

"Yay." Slade's cheer came out in a breathless whisper. It had hurt more than he wanted to admit, climbing into Lance's lap. "We should go home where I have a ring waiting on you. Then I can show you all the ways we can touch that it doesn't hurt."

"Excuse me, Mr. O'Neil. This is a—"

Slade cut off the server by handing the guy his black card. "Everyone's lunch is on me," Slade yelled for everyone to hear. "This one just agreed to marry me."

The cheering and commotion his announcement caused canceled out his inelegant behavior when Lance had accepted, as far as Slade was concerned. Slade sat sideways on Lance's lap, letting people congratulate them and soaking up the way Lance stroked his back until the server returned with his card and receipt. He barely spared a glance for the two-hundred-thousand-dollar total before tipping the guy eighty thousand dollars and signing the receipt.

He met Lance's stare. "Can we go home now?"

With a nod, Lance stood. He let Slade's feet slide to the ground only long enough to move from behind the table. Then he grabbed Slade's ass and lifted as Slade wrapped around him like a monkey. Lance carried Slade from the restaurant without showing an ounce of shame. Slade couldn't love a man more. They were happy. His heart was full.

*

The numbness from the shock didn't fully lift until Lance walked into their bedroom and Slade slipped a ring on Lance's finger. It turned out he had bought matching engagement rings and wedding bands for them several months ago. They were intricately designed with music notes carved on the wider wedding bands. Slade said when the notes were played, they would sound like, "I love you." As always, Lance had never been more blown away by anyone. The last few weeks had washed away the ugly moments. Slade treated Lance like a king despite being the one who needed care. Lance didn't think he could be happier, and then Slade worked on stripping Lance.

Slade kissed Lance deep while pulling at his clothes. He let Slade have each piece as they made their way to the bed. The moment Lance sat nude on the edge of the mattress with Slade between his knees, he went to work on Slade's clothes. He moved slow. Slade's body was still one huge bruise. While his skin had gone from black to yellow, Lance knew Slade still lived in constant pain. Lance wanted to make him feel good. That was why he tried to let Slade lead.

Once their bare skin brushed, Slade shoved at Lance's chest, urging him onto his back before straddling his body. Lance nearly snapped with Slade's ass right where he needed him. It felt like forever since he had last made love to Slade. The longing was torture.

"You look so beautiful." Slade kissed Lance's chest. "There's so much love and hunger in your expression that I'm blown away by you."

Lance gasped for air as Slade reached between them and adjusted their erections so they would stroke each other as Slade's hips rolled. He didn't respond until he caught his breath. "I can't imagine I ever look at you any other way."

Slade braced his hands on the mattress on either side of Lance. He stared down at Lance, boldly holding his gaze as he made love to Lance with no penetration. "You've looked at me with emptiness and hatred before. It ripped out my heart."

Lance's lungs froze.

Slade wasn't finished. "You looked at me like a stranger and like I could cheat."

"No." The word tore from Lance, ripping at his vocal cords. Slade remembered. That had been his biggest fear when he talked to Slade about those pictures, but it had been too important to avoid.

Slade kissed him. Their tongues stroked. The pressure in Lance's chest eased. Slade had still asked Lance to marry him and still made love to him. Lance had to cling to the hope in that.

"I love you," Slade whispered between kisses. "I shouldn't have driven away. I should have stayed and fought."

Despite being on fire, Lance still fought tears.

"No. I love you so much. I shouldn't have let you go. You deserved better from me." Despite his best efforts, a tear slipped from the corner of Lance's eye and slid back into his hair. He kissed Slade harder as Slade moved faster against him. Their movements and kisses turned frenzied as they stroked and touched, doing whatever it took to get closer to orgasm. Lance couldn't get past the knowledge that Slade remembered the day of his accident. Yet he still asked Lance to marry him. Lance had been so cold and unbending. He didn't deserve this life.

"I didn't earn you," Slade whispered, mimicking Lance's thoughts except in the wrong direction. "I don't deserve the amazing way you treat me."

A roar of aggravation tore from Lance's throat.

179

"Fuck that. You're mine and you're perfect. I don't want anything or anyone else. I couldn't love anyone more." Lance scratched at the sheets to keep from digging his fingers into Slade's bruised skin. "Fuck. You make me insane. I want to spend the rest of my life just like this."

"Wish granted." Slade sat back on his heels and palmed their cocks, stroking and riding his hand until Lance thought his mind would snap. His muscles tensed. Lance held his breath. He focused on the building pleasure. Ecstasy slammed into him. A cry tore from his throat as cum coated his body. Lance didn't know if was only his or a combination of their fluids. He couldn't think straight enough to do anything but ride the high.

Slade collapsed onto Lance's chest, obviously uncaring of the mess. Lance tilted Slade's chin up and claimed his lips. They were breathless and fought for air around each other's tongue. To Lance, it was the perfect kiss. They hadn't been the perfect relationship everyone dreamed of having, but they were real. Lance knew in his heart they would fight for each other for the rest of their lives, no matter the battle. Goddamn. He couldn't believe Slade recalled that ugly fight and still asked Lance to marry him. Lance didn't know what he had done to deserve this second shot at a life with Slade, but he knew they wouldn't squander it. They were solid and beautiful. No one would work harder than them. Lance couldn't wait to see what happened next. He was ridiculously in love with an awkward and somewhat clumsy rock star. It was amazing. He was humbled, but he was also home.

Chapter Nine

For the millionth time in Cade's life, he wondered if he was a terrible person. It always seemed as if every decision he made came to a crossroads of what was considered moral. Then he chose the wrong path. Felix hadn't come to Slade and Lance's wedding. Cade had known ahead of time he wouldn't show. The pictures of them on his phone that Felix's wife had sent to him had proven that. The kicker was, Cade hadn't known he was married. They had meant nothing to Cade. Sometimes, Felix had said and done things that led Cade to believe Felix was falling in love and Cade should run for the hills. If he had known about a wife, Cade would like to think he wouldn't have messed with Felix. Honestly, though, he didn't know. Felix was sexy and willing to do anything. Cade could close his eyes and picture anyone while Felix gave him whatever he begged for. It had been simple. Everything else was complicated.

Cade watched as Slade kissed Lance like no one could see them. Some of the biggest stars milled around the reception, catching up and pretending they didn't see the happy couple's private moment. Cade couldn't look away. He had almost lost his brother. Cade thought about that a lot. His guilty conscience made him feel like it was somehow his fault. The universe had tried teaching him a lesson by stealing away his only family. Message received.

Terrell King, the pitcher for the L.A. Direwolves, appeared at Cade's side with two glasses of champagne. He held one out to Cade before claiming the empty seat at his side. Cade accepted with a smile. He ran into Terrell occasionally. They ran in the same circles. That was the thing about being Slade's twin. He was always surrounded by famous people, but he wasn't really one of them. Terrell had come from nothing to become one of the biggest names in baseball. He never ignored Cade the way most people did.

"So, does Slade know you're in love with his new husband?"

Cade shot Terrell a panicked look. "What?"

A wicked-looking smile briefly touched Terrell's lips. His mismatched gaze—one blue eye and one brown—latched on to Cade with a knowing stare. He sipped his drink as if he hadn't guessed Cade's biggest and most shameful secret.

Cade decided to be an ass. "You shouldn't start ugly rumors like that. My brother is all I have. Not everyone can afford to lose their only family."

A cruel smile touched Terrell's lips. He looked like he ran his tongue over his teeth beneath his lips. "Damn. I must've really hit the nail on the head if I rated that low of a blow."

Completely at odds with his personality, Cade felt guilty. Everyone knew Terrell had been raised by an adoptive family who used him for his talent, hoping he would make them rich. They had adopted him as a teenager who was already on his way to a huge career. Terrell had cut them from his life and never looked back. They had done several interviews, grasping for public pity. People were divided on whether Terrell was an ungrateful piece of shit or in the right. Cade had always believed the latter.

Before Cade could apologize, Lance led Slade

185

onto the dance floor for their first dance. Cade fought the urge to watch Lance's every move like a lovesick fool. It wasn't anyone's fault. Slade had been too busy for them. They had spent too much time together. Cade had caught feelings he didn't want. It was a story Cade would take to his grave. More couples joined them on the floor.

Terrell plucked the glass from Cade's hand and set it aside. "Dance with me."

Since Terrell wasn't telling him he was a piece of shit, Cade accepted. Once he found himself in Terrell's arms, Cade's mind shifted gears. He didn't know why he hadn't expected Terrell to be so hard beneath his clothes, but goddamn. His shoulders were definitely distracting. Cade found his gaze latching on to Terrell's. Terrell stared back at him as if he had been waiting for Cade's attention. Once he had it, his mouth lifted in one corner in a ridiculously sexy smirk.

"Damn."

Cade had no idea what Terrell's sexy curse had been about, but butterflies stirred in his stomach. It seemed the night wasn't the complete nightmare he had expected after all. He was already ready to fuck his life up with someone new. Terrell looked like a good choice.

*

Lance still couldn't believe how quickly and easily his wedding with Slade had come together. For him, it had been a no brainer to get married right away. Everything had gone as smoothly as possible—like the universe had given them its blessing. Their first dance together as a married couple had him incapable of taking his eyes off Slade. He still couldn't believe this was his husband.

Slade smiled. It was sweet and filled with wonder. "You're my husband." Slade said the words as if he was every bit as mystified as Lance.

"Damn right." Lance held Slade even tighter and claimed his lips. Love choked him. He had never been happier. Maybe they hadn't had the perfect love story, but they were still flawless in Lance's eyes and he couldn't be happier. The music came to an end. Lance didn't want to let him go, but Slade pulled away. His eyes flashed with mischief.

"I still have a few surprises left for you."

Before Lance could ask what he meant, Slade jogged toward the stage where the band stood and commandeered the microphone. The band didn't look surprised. That was Lance's first clue this had been planned.

"Hey guys. Don't leave the dance floor. I have another slow song for you. This one is releasing on my upcoming album." As he spoke, someone switched out Slade's microphone for a wireless one on a headpiece. Slade leaped off the stage while still speaking to their guests. "I wrote this one while on tour and thousands of miles away from the most patient and understanding man on the planet." Slade held Lance's stare while he walked into his arms. "I love you, baby. You've put up with a lot, but you mean everything to me. This one is called *Awkward Love*."

A smile exploded across Lance's face as the band started playing and Slade sang. They slow danced and Lance absorbed every word. His eyes burned, but he refused to close them against the sight of Slade singing to him. Every word was perfect. Slade sang about no one else seeing him as the mess he was offstage. He sang the story of Lance loving the real him that no one else knew. Slade completely bared his soul about the loneliness of fame and the fake version of him that didn't exist outside of music. He sang about Lance in a way Lance had never seen himself. It was humbling and had tears gathering in Lance's eyes. Lance hadn't known people loved like this until he had fallen. He knew one thing, though. Lance would love and treasure Slade for the rest of his life. They had already survived good times and bad. Sickness and health. There was nothing that could break them now. They were perfect.

Please keep an eye out for the next Candied Crush, *Beautifully Wicked* (http://mybook.to/BeautifullyWicked).

Please consider leaving a review at the retailer where you purchased this book. Reviews really help with a book's visibility, which allows me to continue writing more stories. Thank you, Charity.

About the Author

Charity Parkerson is an award-winning and multi-published author with several companies. Born with no filter from her brain to her mouth, she decided to take this odd quirk and insert it in her characters.

*Eight-time Readers' Favorite Award Winner
*2015 Passionate Plume Award Finalist
*2013 Reviewers' Choice Award Winner
*2012 ARRA Finalist for Favorite Paranormal Romance
*Five-time winner of The Mistress of the Darkpath

Connect with her online:

—Sign up for my newsletter:
https://sendfox.com/charityparkerson
http://bit.ly/CharityNews
—Join my readers' group on Facebook:
http://bit.ly/CharitysTribe
—Website: charityparkerson.com
—Facebook:
facebook.com/authorCharityParkerson
facebook.com/TheMenofSin
—Twitter: twitter.com/CharityParkerso

—Instagram:
Instagram.com/sinnerauthor
—Bookbub:
https://www.bookbub.com/authors/cha
rity-parkerson
—Amazon page:
author.to/CharityParkerson
(http://author.to/CharityParkerson)